HATCHING STONES

Anna Wilson

Published in 1991 by Onlywomen Press Ltd.
Radical Feminist Lesbian publishers,
38 Mount Pleasant, London WC1X 0AP

Printed and bound by Billing & Sons, Worcester, U.K.
Typeset in Melior by Columns, Reading, Berkshire, U.K.

British Library Cataloguing in Publication data
Wilson, Anna 1954
  Hatching stones.
  I. Title
  823.914 [F]
  ISBN 0–906500–39–7

for sophie

This is clearly a work of fiction.
For, as we know, there are no bears in the
antarctic.

CONTENTS

*"There is no document of civilization which is not at the
same time a document of barbarism"* Walter Benjamin.
Theses on the Philosophy of History

Section 1: The History of Initial Events

Chapter 1

The technology came first, as is usually the case, and was threatening to become fully operational and change the shape of the world before anyone had had time to consider how it could be used, or how controlled. Genetic engineering itself – on some pre-human level – had long been taken for granted as a useful means of producing a disease-resistant grain or a leaner breed of sheep. The sudden possibility of producing humans, however, seemed to take even those responsible for the successful experiments by surprise. Once the word was out there followed a period of intense speculation: airwaves and newsprint were choked with wild theories of the discovery's significance, and wilder fantasies about the future of the human race. This period of shock and adjustment ended abruptly; people shook off their paralysis and began to seek out and apply the new technique to themselves. Within three months there were clinics claiming to have access to the new technology in every major city, a network of back street operators, and the threat of a population explosion on a scale never envisaged in modern times. The government of Lelaki, having failed to foresee any of these problems, sought to make amends by putting an immediate moratorium on the whole process. It then retired into frightened conference to decide how the world was to be brought back from the brink of chaos.

The fundamentals of the problem lay in the technology being a means not of producing human beings as it were from nothing, but rather a means of reproducing them. If one had a body it was now readily possible to produce several more from it; and this with the new practice still in its infancy. It was not difficult to foresee the day when a single body could be reproduced into an army. There would, it was true, continue to be a time lag of sorts, given that the new humans were produced (after their nine months of growth in controlled foetal nutrition environments) as newborn babies rather than adults. But in essence it was now within the capacity of anyone to reproduce themselves a private army. In fifteen years, it was said, the streets would be murderous with teenage gangs of warring youth.

No one in government had even foreseen the lure to the ordinary person of the power to reproduce a simulacrum of themselves. Perhaps they had unconsciously assumed that the poor, the unattractive and the disadvantaged found themselves as undesirable as they seemed to the privileged who wielded power. In fact the country was full of people now desperate to give themselves, as magically reproduced, the advantages and chances they had never had. The social consequences of this might have been advantageous, in as much as people's attention was diverted from their own situation. The country might look forward to an era of particular placidity while the nation struggled quietly on behalf of its youthful replicated selves. But it had also to be considered that should everyone's second chance not succeed, should it become clear that there was no future for their new selves just as there had not been for the old, a surge of rage and rebellion might easily rise up and tear the social fabric thread from thread.

The problem did not, of course, end with an individual's desire to see himself grow up under his own protection. It had begun to dawn on those in power that all those who saw themselves as weak, unsupported, as a lone voice crying unheard, might seek to make themselves more a force to be reckoned with by creating as many identical reproductions of themselves as they could. And it was hard to assume that the need for a couple of decades' lead time for one's plan to come to fruition would be sufficient disincentive for all acts of revenge. The pleasure of being able to send round thirty of yourself to get your own back if someone insulted you in the street might, some pessimists felt, be considered worth waiting for.

The inter-state conference was scheduled to last a week, though as they ran up the steps from their cars the governors tended to say bravely that they'd be there as long as it took. It seemed at first as if it would take no time at all; it was merely a question of detailing the ways in which prohibition would be enforced, and of deciding what would be done with any illegal offspring that came into the hands of the law. They were in session on the second afternoon, arguing over whether it would be safer to segregate seized offspring from other children, when someone pointed out that to ban the one thing that everyone in the country most wanted to do would surely bring down the government. There was a pause: some drank water, others lit cigarettes. Someone else remarked that really no one could be blamed for wanting to be able to predict what their child would look like; ordinary – women's – babies were so various and unreliable. Around the table, they knew he was thinking of his own daughter, stupid, intractable and promiscuous.

Once the subject had been broached there seemed no stopping them: they all began to confide to their neighbours their secret hopes of a child of their own, and to voice their secret thoughts of the new technology's advantages. Suddenly they were in confusion and could reach no conclusions; they grasped longingly at a vision of a new world, only to draw back hurriedly for fear of burning themselves in the white heat of its power to overturn their lives.

The meeting dragged on; the waiting newsmen were told only that the problem was difficult, that they were devoting themselves to its solution. At last they were able to drag themselves away from the intoxicating prospect of a different future sufficiently at least to consider what it was exactly that attracted them and therefore, they assumed, the rest of the country. (Even then, they were vaguely aware that the rest of the world regarded the new technology, with curious

4

unanimity, as an abomination and a threat. But their sense of national moral superiority was enough, at least for the moment, to render this fact of little concern.) What finally the attraction, when they looked at it, seemed to come down to was the predictability of this new specie of offspring, its sameness, the familiarity that a parent felt at the sight of his small self. For a while they were able only to hold this fact in their hands, to turn it this way and that, not knowing the use or significance of it, not knowing what they were to do with it.

There were visiting scientists in attendance, summoned in case they should be needed to explain the inner workings of their troublesome skill, or how easy it really would be to duplicate it illegally. The President turned to one of these men, at length, and asked whether an offspring had to be an exact replica of oneself, or whether one couldn't tinker with the genes a little — to eradicate, say, some niggling hereditary defect. He was thinking only that he had never liked the shape of his ears, had always felt they spoilt his profile, and would have liked to be able to reproduce himself with a less cumbersome pair. The scientist looked at him, surprised. It was hard to remember that these were men who did not know these simple details, did not know them because they were already powerful enough to feel the urge to renew themselves less strongly than did others; their names, by and large, were not on the waiting lists of the illicit but expensive clinics in the capital city. Certainly, he said, it was possible to make changes to the gene pattern. Very few people were without something that they wanted to change — those of less than average height, for example, asked for their offspring to be taller by a few inches; women often wanted theirs to have a somewhat different body shape. So they don't really have to be copies of their fathers at all, the President murmured.

That day the conference mapped out a scheme whereby clients of the new technology would be obliged to have offspring of a range of different types. Every family would be mixed, and from this would

5

come an inevitable breakdown of prejudice and racial hatred. Looking down into the cradle that held something that he recognised as uniquely his own, his thoughts and fears as well as his flesh and blood, a parent would see only beauty in a difference of skin tone. The plan would usher in a new era of tolerance and understanding.

They had now reached the end of the week scheduled for the conference, and it was thought wiser to allow the governors home to deal with any problems that had arisen in their absence. Several state legislatures seemed to be taking advantage of their governor's temporary departure to introduce inconsistent and arbitrary emergency regulations on the very subject that the conference was in the midst of addressing. There was a mood of uncertainty and of covert challenge to authority abroad; the President and his governors, in all the glory of their elected office and their absolute powers, were in danger of being ignored by the little people of the local assemblies. Action must be swift: the meeting was to reconvene for a final determination at the end of a week. During those seven days away the governors had the opportunity to consult their friends and advisors clandestinely about the plan, and found it overwhelmingly rejected. Indeed, once away from the otherworldly expansiveness of the conference table, they themselves began to wonder how they could have agreed, even provisionally, to such a scheme. Their brief vision of harmony was transformed into a nightmare of dissent, a perverse denial of the self-fulfillment that the new technology offered, a ghastly blueprint for the painful reenactment of social hierarchy in every home.

And yet when the conference reconvened the President clung to his plan. The meeting split into factions and there was a violent backlash from some, who were now against allowing any use of the new technology at all. There was a flaw, the dissenters claimed, in the whole scheme: why did everyone assume that their offspring, just because they looked so like them, just because they emanated from their own flesh, would turn out the same at all, they asked.

6

Surely a boy who looked just like his father, who knew in fact that he was just like his father, would be all the more determined to rebel, to depart as much as possible from the parental pattern. The new technology, in other words, would be an instrument of social chaos. The President walked in the windy garden with the scientists, picking their brains for a means to shore up his utopian scheme. What he needed was a glimpse of the future. The first babies of the new boom were only three months old, and if the reports were that they were a tractable lot, the sceptics pointed out that they were unusually well-cared for, as well as being too young to mouth obscenities at their doting parents. When it seemed that the President was alone in his faith, and that nothing could stop the governors combining together to demand a ban, the scientists, seeing their beautiful life's work about to be condemned, produced their own offspring, the firstborn. Summoned from their various schools and colleges, the boys ranged in age from nine to twenty, the eldest the very first fruits of their fathers' experiments.

Only the offspring of the top three scientists were there; as the pioneers they naturally had the oldest products, the ones most likely to be useful to the President's cause. They were clearly identifiable as their fathers' children: standing in sibling groups around each adult, the resemblance was shocking. Aside from this disturbing quality, the governors found, questioning them, a group of nice, thoughtful, responsible youths. Though they pried and harried the eldest ones, they could find only the smallest signs of adolescent rebellion, signs without which they might have questioned the normality of the young men's development. The boys were willing to challenge their fathers' opinions in the light of new ideas, but they seemed to feel no need to destroy or undermine them merely in order to establish their own identity. They appeared confident of themselves as individuals while cheerfully acknowledging their fathers in them.

There seemed no escaping the conclusion that they were a very desirable, if at once slightly different and slightly conservative, set of offspring. Their fathers, attempting to explain this phenomenon to the governors, said that it was as if their fathers' attitudes had by some means leached into the genes from which the boys were reproduced. Hesitantly, they suggested that a child formed from the division of an adult cell was constructed from material that had mutated in some way that an ordinary embryo, creating as it did a fresh combination, did not duplicate. The heretical implications of this theory to the existing science of genetics hardly impinged on the governors' thoughts; it was not impossible for them to imagine that every cell in their body knew, in some sense, what they themselves knew. The hypothesis was borne out, the scientists said, by studies of the boys' development as young children. Knowledge already acquired by their fathers before the children were born was much easier for these boys to acquire in their turn than for ordinary children of the same age. But they found other kinds of learning, those not part of their fathers' knowledge, as hard to learn as the average child. They were not, overall, either more or less intelligent than their fathers, but perhaps because learning of some sorts came readily to them, they seemed more confident, less under stress; they had an innate confidence of being able at least to equal their parent's level of achievement.

The boys' appearance turned some tide; the governors wavered again between the torrent of change that threatened to carry them and all they knew away, and the dam that could maintain stability, and with it, stagnation. The President, an unimaginative man, managed a rare leap of faith, searching in his desperation for a way to salvage something of his impossible dream of a nation unified. He had noticed, as had they all, the boys' extraordinary resemblance to their fathers. Although he had grown used to the phenomenon, it continued to strike him that it was really very incongruous that these offspring, so much a step towards a more perfect world in many ways, should be saddled with their fathers' random, and often not especially pleasing, physiognomy. How much better it would have been, he felt, if one of the scientists had not seen fit to replicate his own rather orange hair and overly fair skin; no one could disagree, he felt, that a slight movement toward the ideal would have been no loss and a considerable gain for the boys themselves and for all who had to do with them.

His idea was introduced to the governors, weary of conflict as they were, their assumptions about the world unhinged by the sight of those quiet, normal-seeming anomalies, by the junior scientist on the team. A youthful, unassuming man, he talked quietly on, cheerfully taking account of every suggestion, until the conference found that it had agreed to a plan breathtaking in its implications. He asked them, first, to acknowledge the palpable truth that certain characteristics, mental, psychological, physical, were generally considered desirable by every intelligent, socially responsible citizen. He listed a few of these and they nodded; the following remarks, to the effect that they would all like to be able to predict and thus control the quality of their offspring, were uncontentious after their days spent facing these truths. And surely they would like their sons to measure up to that common ideal, the young man continued, pausing while the governors allowed a visual image to float before them, an image so often in considerable contrast to the reality that awaited them in their acrimonious homes. Feeling the receptivity of his audience, the President took over the exposition of the plan: they would gather together a composite picture of what the nation as a whole thought the most desirable properties of the national character, and they would allow citizens to produce an offspring or two per family who contained a few, though not all, of these attributes. There would only be a limited amount of genetic engineering. The offspring would be very like their parent, but they would be significantly better. They would be improved, more like everyone wished their children to be. In a few years, the country as a whole would have changed for the better; people would be more like each other and so they would like each other more.

The details were sorted out within the next few

9

days. In the interest of fairness there would be an enormous and costly referendum to determine, down to the last fraction of an inch or tone of skin colour or degree of introversion, what it was the people wanted. And then, and the governors were awestruck by the grandeur and simplicity of their scheme, they were going to get it. The results would of course be carefully tabulated before being assessed and adapted by the genetic engineers' panel of experts to ensure that the ideal to be attained in the distant future of several generations was, by all scientific and humanist criteria, a whole human being.

The President's media advisors, brought in to draft the speeches and mock up the videos that would electrify the country with a vision of a unique future, worried about minority groups, whose preferences might be submerged by a composite ideal, or whose values might on the other hand produce an unexpected slant to the statistics. It was suggested that a few alternative models might be drawn up for ethnic minorities to work toward; but the conference rejected the notion as a misconception of their scheme, indeed as denying the very heart of its guiding principle. The people wanted unity, not difference; and the governors felt confident that their constituents' dreams for themselves and for their country were very similar to those articulated by their elected officials. They believed that the ideal would turn out to be shared in common – a child that anyone would be proud to acknowledge as their own.

To a large extent, the results of the survey – meticulously delivered to and collected from every adult, notwithstanding the expense and difficulty of such an undertaking – bore out this optimistic prediction of unanimity. Living as they did in a society where the values of the majority were more or less unchallengeable, so natural and comfortable did they seem, a large proportion of many minorities gave a description of their ideal child and future citizen that differed not at all from that offered by the President himself, down to the sunny blond of his hair. There were those who clung to the traditional

values of their community and who thus delivered
ideals that were, physically at least, and sometimes
even psychologically, widely different from the norm.
Perhaps because of this small but vociferous element,
the ideal that finally began to emerge from the
engineers' panel had an interesting bronze tint to his
skin and a warmth of manner somewhat foreign to
most ruling classes. This was not enough in itself to
prevent some active and discontented elements from
attempting to contest, or to persuade their groups to
withdraw from, the offspring project. But dissenters
found their own communities divided against them,
most seeing the new technology as the means by
which minorities might finally participate on equal
terms in the future of the nation. Their offspring
would be their fathers' sons, members of the community of their birth, after all – and at least to start
with they wouldn't look so very different either; and
to refuse to participate would be to consign themselves to a backward and marginalized future, to a
repetition of the past. Only the most radical of the
objectors, foreseeing the destruction of their culture in
the coming homogenization, were determined enough
to leave the country, seeking sanctuary in other
continents whose governments had condemned the
new technology as ungodly and dangerous. Bound
together in a common purpose, the nation saw them
leave without regret.

Chapter 2

The infrastructure necessary to administer and oversee the new technology was in place within months of the results of the national referendum being made known. Schedules and lotteries were introduced to minimize the dip in production caused by the enormous increase in requests for paternity leave and reduced working hours made by new parents. The country single-mindedly set about having babies.

The regulations drawn up by the governors allowed for each individual to make a choice between having a child the usual – or, as it quickly became known, the old way – or having an offspring under the new technology. Thus, after a certain date, those who chose either method were debarred from using the other; this in order to ensure that there would be no unmanageable rise in the population. As the potential child-bearing population had more than quadrupled overnight, no one was to have more than one child of any origin unless an existing one died. It soon became clear that almost no one deliberately opted for the old way when they could start their family on the way towards the ideal of tomorrow. Men whose wives or girlfriends happened to get pregnant would persuade them into abortions, or disown them, rather than miss the chance of an offspring of their own – for it had been decided that biological fatherhood of the old-fashioned, indirect, sort counted (as after all it had always done before) as having a child for the purposes of the regulations. The governors' legal staff had advised this on the grounds that men might otherwise be inclined to disclaim, or cease to maintain, the children of their wives. Fewer 'natural' babies were born each year.

The problem of women's increasing redundancy as child-bearers turned out, in fact, to have wider dimensions, to be the least of their problems in the long run. The ideal that the country had voted for had, after all, been a masculine one. Most women, perhaps from force of habit, had depicted their ideal citizen as a man. Perhaps they had not fully realized that they could not have a male offspring by the new technology, the possibility of manipulating genes having apparently led the public erroneously to assume that it would be an equally simple matter to manipulate chromosomes. Given that it was a unified ideal that was being sought, no blueprint for the woman of the future had, therefore, been drawn up. Women were, for the moment, excluded from participation in the new way. A few doom-sayers had begun to remark that unless something was done or unless the novelty wore off and the rate of ordinary pregnancies increased, native-born women would successively become first rare, then ageing curiosities, and finally extinct.

The President's memoirs, dictated as an old man in his summer house in the verdant hills of the north, are surprisingly frank on the subject. He admits disarmingly that he had not really considered the problem of what to do about women, and that the crisis that suddenly came upon him some ten years after the nation's method of birth management had changed was entirely unexpected. Everyone – even his wife, whom he counted as among his most valued advisors – had assumed that a considerable proportion of the population would continue to copulate and reproduce in the usual way. This did, of course, go on, especially at first. But as the oldest of the 'new' children began to grow up, and were discernibly so much better behaved and well-adjusted than the other sort, men without children began to avoid intercourse with fertile women with an extraordinary persistence and self-control.

Family life had begun to fracture. While there were very few girls of less than ten years of age, women were naturally still normally represented across the remainder of the age range, and hence families retained much their usual composition. But those men who had not yet been successful in the lottery and who were therefore still waiting for their chance for an offspring of their own, avoiding the fertility of their wives, or any woman who might claim them as the father of a child, began to look on women primarily as dangerous. It was an attitude that gradually spread, affecting those who, already blessed by an offspring, had tended rather to ignore than to fear their wives. Women, finding themselves and their babies rejected, shut out from the future of the nation, discovered themselves hating their husbands, the government, men everywhere, for having, as they saw it, tricked them into giving up their rightful place in the world. It was not long before reports started to collect showing that women were often venting their rage on the helpless new offspring, the usurper in every home. It began to be suggested that women would soon no longer be psychologically suitable as rearers, that they would have to be disbarred even from this traditional rôle.

Women organized themselves into political groups and campaigned for a return to the old methods of birth. Others demanded a female version of the ideal to allow women to participate directly in the future of the country. Activist cells formed and raided now neglected sperm banks; there was a sudden increase in natural births of little girls.

The President, finally abandoning the idea that he could ride out the demographic glitch until safely elected for a third term, called another conference. Officially to review the progress of the new technology ten years on, it was obvious to commentators everywhere that the problem of women would be the major item under discussion. It might have been expected that the meeting would take place in an atmosphere of tension, given the urgency of the crisis, the possible threat to the stability of the entire birth programme. In fact the governors appeared confident and relaxed. This phenomenon could perhaps be explained by the circumstance of this being one of those occasions, now become commonplace, when a creche and tutoring facilities were laid on for the governors' children. Although such provision was thought desirable in case some governors did not feel confident leaving their offspring in the care of their wives, it also reflected the degree of interest and involvement usually felt by fathers of the 'new children'. Most governors requested a suite of rooms to facilitate their spending the time remaining to them, when conference was not in session, with their sons.

In any event, the mood of the first session was calm and determined; the men present were deeply committed to what was at stake. The initial consensus was inclined to be pragmatic: they would safeguard the process without diluting it too significantly if they were to allow those women who chose to do so to reproduce a female version of the ideal citizen. It was widely accepted that this concession would largely end feminine agitation for a return to natural methods, the results of which the governors were unanimous in finding inferior, or at least retrogressive. And it seemed obvious that Adam needed his Eve to fulfil those obligations and attributes that had always, with minor historical variations, been women's lot. The governors congratulated themselves on being both responsive to, and able to encompass, the woman's point of view, the political accidents that had ensured that no woman had been governor of a state for forty years notwithstanding.

The establishment of a female ideal also provided a solution to the problem of sex, an important consideration for the men gathered about that oval table, many of whose own sons (high office enabling one to jump the offspring queue) would soon be prepubescent no longer. The governors spent a mildly ribald afternoon discussing the ideal breast, and arguing as to whether women themselves could be trusted to aim for what men would prefer. And yet there was something about this discussion that rang false; despite their pretension to stag night bonhomie, an observant and dispassionate fly on the wall of that room might have decided that they did not, at bottom, really care what shape a feminine ideal might take. Already a rather male-identified culture, the nation had become gradually more identified with traditionally masculine values over the past few years. This could be traced in part to the effect of the new offsprings' being male: not only did the future seem, albeit inadvertently, to be gendered male, but the fact that in practice the law allowed only men to benefit from the new technology had given all men, as potential fathers of offspring, additional prestige and self-assurance.

The culture had acquired, in addition, a profound distrust of women in general. Perhaps a submerged feeling had merely been allowed to surface: but the combination of a fear of natural children being produced, out of order, by women insisting on the right to motherhood, and the female discontent that had begun to take form, threatening even the lives of the offspring, the nation's hope and joy, had led to men avoiding the company of women. The governors' conference thus only duplicated on a higher social plane a movement that was evident in all walks of life – men worked, played and often even – especially if they had already been lucky and had a child – lived and shared child-care together. Without the thought being made explicit, there was thus a subtext to the governors' light-hearted discussion: could they, any longer, actually believe in a female ideal? Would not such a being seem a pale shadow of her brother, viewed by him with indifference or contempt, a source of dissatisfaction even to herself? Playing chess with their sons in the evening, or hanging fondly over their cots, the governors found their vision of a new world hard to reconcile with a dilution of the dream.

It was only after another seventy-two hours of inconsequential discussion, of idle banter and circular reasoning, that the conference began explicitly to consider finding a solution to the current problem that did not involve legislating for the research and establishment of a female model offspring to match the male one. Even then, the enormity of the step they contemplated was not overtly on the table. Rather the

governors concentrated on the immediate consequences for their offspring of an absence of young
women – the problem of sex. This they considered
squarely. It was impossible to reconcile the better lives
they foresaw for their sons with their being obliged,
for lack of female partners, to become homosexual.
Bizarre alternative schemes began to circulate. Most of
these involved relatively few women, produced by
natural means, who would be sexually available to
large groups of men. Or perhaps it would be necessary
for their sons to go overseas (overseas travel was
difficult, since the new technology, but not impossible). On the other hand, perhaps genetic engineering
should be used to produce a few specially adapted
females. All these alternatives seemed to the governors
sordid and abhorrent. They wondered whether the
men of the future might not, eventually, be sufficiently
self-disciplined as to be able to endure celibacy, and
whether this would be a sacrifice or an advance.

It is unclear whether the scientists felt that a sight
of their offspring would provide an answer to the
governors' dilemma, or whether they only thought that
a reunion with the pioneers of the new way might lift
their spirits. In the event their arrival brought about a
breakthrough, just as it had ten years before. They
came into the room in a body, the eldest of them
bringing with them sons of their own. It was
interesting to note that, as they had matured, siblings
had grown less alike – or perhaps the governors had
only become more attuned to subtle distinctions. They
laid their hands on each other's shoulders and smiled,
and the governors felt impelled to smile back, as
warmed as if they themselves had been responsible for
their creation.

Soon the meeting had broken up into small groups,
each centered around one of the offspring, and all
discussing the problem of sexual partners for the
future. No doubt the offspring had been warned of the
topic uppermost in the governors' minds; at any rate
they set about explaining to their audience that no
allowances had as yet been made for the effects on
them of having been produced in another's image, and

of their intending to continue this process themselves. They said that while they felt, of course, the usual human need to perpetuate the species, for them this was quite divorced, logically and emotionally, from any sexual activity. The governors were not surprised by this, of course, given the now long-established disassociation of sex from reproduction; the earnest young offspring assured them, however, that they spoke of something quite different in degree – of a complete absence of the inchoate, unconscious urge. They then demanded of their listeners that they list the satisfactions that they sought from sexual relationships. When they had set aside the responses that had to do with affection, understanding, commitment and the like, on the grounds that they sought and obtained these things from their brothers and offspring friends, and much more readily so than other people for having so much in common with them, there remained only those things relating to the physical act of sex itself. For sensual satisfaction, the young men said, they found physical contact that was not directly sexual very satisfactory. It had already become apparent to the governors that these young men were more physical with one another than was ordinary, at least within their culture. And as far as intercourse is concerned, they continued, we find that fantasy provides us with all the company we need in any sex act. Cross-examined by their graceful interlocutors, the governors admitted that they were of course familiar with such fantasies, and often themselves found them more fulfilling than what they were in the habit of thinking of as the real thing. The young men then confessed that they appeared not to require as much sexual activity as the original sort of human (with whom they had of course had considerable contact, even while they found the society of other offspring more congenial). They speculated that their reduced need might be connected to an apparently happier and less problematic emotional life. The next generation, they suggested, could be expected to carry this trend further.

It was not until many years later that it emerged, or

18

was inferred, that the offspring had not chosen to tell the whole truth about themselves at that crucial meeting. It seems that, having noticed some years previously, as the first substantial group of their sort reached their mid-teens, that their sexual inclinations tended to be rather different from the average, they had met together to consider what, if anything, was to be done about it, and what, if anything, should be said to curious observers. They agreed then that they saw nothing undesirable in their habits, but that it would be politic not to allow details to emerge in public.

The fact was that they were a great deal more sexually active than they allowed the governors to know, correctly supposing that details of their preference for sex in groups, and their taking little account of which of them were siblings in these activities, would probably have persuaded the governors to introduce women into the programme at once, or at least to alter radically the upbringing given to the new children. The offspring would appear to have seen themselves, already, as having a duty to the new generations of offspring unborn, a duty that overrode their loyalty to their fathers or the old order. The governors, on the other hand, were committed to the new world that the offspring offered; they wanted to trust them. Although they came away from that meeting with a new sense of having begun the process of creating a kind of man who would be more different from themselves than they had either envisaged or intended, this slight feeling of a loss of control was not enough in itself to cause them to lose faith.

One of the first offspring, asked to reminisce in his old age about his peer group's apparent lack of interest in having female companions of like sort provided for them, seemed rueful but unashamed. "You must not blame us," he said. "We were our fathers' children. We were only able to articulate on a logical plane what our fathers' generation must always have felt or wanted to be allowed to feel." The young man interviewing him noted down the signs of inwardness, his subject's return to the past in memory, in the silence that followed. "And then, we were a very

19

tightly-knit, defensive little group. Of course we loved each other."

Once it had become apparent that no room was to be made in the new world of the future for the women of the country (although this was not, as yet, how the decision was formulated), the problem became one of presentation. The men gathered there were naturally aware of the dangers of openly and deliberately disenfranchising – this being the locution that they found most accurate to describe the non-inclusion of women in the privilege of new technology – half the population, even a half so traditionally politically unaware and passive in the face of their destiny. They could hardly dare to hope that this change would pass off with as little disturbance as had the departure of the disaffected sections of the ethnic minorities; women were still so much more entwined in the fabric of their society. And yet this entanglement no longer signified an aspect of society that was inextricable from its most sacred values, but rather a canker that had burrowed its way inconveniently close to the bone. The fear that women would rise up and strike at what the country held most dear, the new children, caused the governors to decide on a course of action that half a generation ago would have been unthinkable. The simple fact that women did not necessarily love and cherish these children made of them a dangerous threat that must be neutralized.

The speeches, when they came, spoke of the hope that women would dedicate themselves to the future of the nation, submerging their individual desires in the greater cause. They spoke of sacrifice and nurturing, and of these traditional female qualities raised to new heights of selflessness. Those whose nobility was not sufficient to this challenge were offered a choice. Mindful of their previous success in ridding themselves of those lacking in patriotic spirit, the governors had had in view to allow women to emigrate, but their tentative enquiries had found no foreign governments willing to take on the burden of what might, after all, turn out to be a very large number of women. It was the President who remembered Baba-i, a large island,

20

theoretically a Lelaki territory, but almost unin-
habited. It lay close enough to the polar icecap to
ensure that any people living on it were obliged to
expend almost all their efforts on merely staying alive.
He was the only one present at the conference who
had visited the place, at some moment when it had
briefly seemed of strategic importance, and he remembered without pleasure a perpetual biting wind, huge
flocks of seabirds, and a few pallid, bony islanders
whose dialect was almost beyond his comprehension.
Those who did not wish to stay and help Lelaki on the
path to greatness were offered free passage to this new,
frontier territory.

There was no mass uprising. Many, terrified by the
prospect of an unknown land where they must grow
old and die, childless, smothered their resentment and
stayed within the family, nanny to the offspring of
their male relatives. Thousands, perhaps hundreds of
thousands, committed suicide. The exact numbers
involved in this epidemic of self-destruction are
unavailable; large quantities of tranquilizers were
readily available at the time, and records, understan-
dably, are incomplete. Some tried to take refuge in the
small fundamentalist communities that had refused to
accept the new technology and that had not seen fit to
leave, though few found permanent refuge there, the
elders fearing the effect on their social structure of
large numbers of unattached women. Others simply
took to the hills and the streets. The women who
remained continued a source of disruption, violence
and unease for some forty years.

The women who left did so in the expectation that
if they stayed they would not be allowed to survive
for long. On the whole the feeling on the great liners
pressed into service to take them to the new land was
that they would likely be torpedoed before they saw
the harbour. The Lelaki government, confident of the
enormous benefit to the nation that their programme
promised, were in fact generous with supplies and the
materials for erecting prefabricated buildings. They
foresaw no need to obliterate the women by force, for
half a century would see the last of them dead, or

certainly past child-bearing age. The President had taken the precaution of having all Lelaki sperm banks destroyed; the women did not carry with them the means to perpetuate themselves.

At home the governors turned their attention to threats from overseas. If they had guided their own people into a positive and moderate use of the new methods, the less did they wish to see the new technology abused by hostile powers in the creation of uncountable armies. Such precautions as they could take against the expertise escaping would doubtless have proved ineffective against any foreign scientist even remotely interested in laying bare the secrets of Lelaki methodology. But other countries seemed oddly reluctant to take the same road; they united instead in international councils to denounce the new technology as unnatural and inhuman, and so profound was their distrust that they appeared to take not even a clandestine interest in putting it to use on any significant scale. It was assumed that the necessary skill was available, and practised occasionally, in the germ warfare laboratories of most industrialized countries, but it was not a virus that ever escaped. With the exile of the women and the escalation of the programme, Lelaki was increasingly condemned and isolated by the international community; that protest remained at a verbal level (ambassadors were withdrawn) when the country rid itself of its alienated women must be assumed to be on account of Lelaki strike capacity, both nuclear and conventional, which was large enough to render any military gesture dangerous – especially, it was felt, since the Lelaki had now to be assumed to be a mentally unbalanced nation. They were left alone, in moral, if not entirely in economic, exile; a period of retreat followed. When the Lelaki reemerged into the global light, it was as a nation transformed, or at least unrecognizable.

*   *   *

22

On the island of Baba-i the women built themselves settlements, herded sheep, trapped birds and, it seemed, waited for death. The original islanders had been airlifted, willingly for the most part, to Lelaki, leaving only the few fertile and intransigent island women behind to explain the seasons, the fishing places, the treacherousness of the surrounding sea. That the Baba-i escaped at last from the hatred and bitterness toward Lelaki that seemed for the first months the only emotion that could survive on that barren rock was due to a small but predictable oversight on the part of the governors of Lelaki. They had not thought that any of the women that they sent away might be, even potentially, genetic engineers; they could see them, by then, only as women, as representatives of the old way, having no knowledge of, or desire for, the new. It took only a short while for a group on the island to assemble the means for the women themselves to produce new offspring. The process of deciding how they should do so, with the spectre of the Lelaki way hanging over them, was long and painful. Eventually, nonetheless, the Baba-i began to be born.

Section 2: Reports from Lelaki

Chapter 1

Jonathan floated. Beneath him starfish of an iridescent, astonishing blue lay tangled together on a rock. The silence was filled only with the sound of his breathing, air rushing and gasping along the tube of his snorkel. When he held his breath there was silence; only the almost-audible beat of the sun on his back, the flicker of a thousand tails as another teeming shoal swirled around him. He floated and smiled for the sheer joy of it, moving his mouth carefully around the mouthpiece for fear of taking a gulp of sea water. The fish twisted on, away from him: he watched as with his movements they took refuge within the coral, their brilliant colours fading into the shade between polyps. Jonathan slowed his limbs until he was hardly resisting the current that pulled him quietly sideways round the bay. Lying so, passive in the arms of the water, he breathed softly and waited for the fish to emerge, taking no more account of him than of some submerged log passing by. And yet always they sensed his presence; to stay with one shoal or another he must always pursue it as it darted away from him.

He idled in the shallows, reluctant to leave the cool water for the undisguised heat of the afternoon sand. He was alone in the shimmering bay; the inhabitants had retreated from the sun. Carefully he imagined the papaya shake that he would order from the shade of the cafe courtyard, the shiver of his flesh as he took a mouthful of the ground ice lying at the bottom of the glass. It was sufficient to carry him up the beach and under the dark of the thatched roof where the beaten earth floor was cold on the soles of his feet. As he sat twirling the straw round his glass, Jonathan wondered at the chance that had brought him here, to this place which anyone would agree was paradise, and with no other responsibilities than to notice anything of interest. His reports were full of the sand quiet in the moonlight, of lying beneath a coconut palm watching fruit bats fly huge and ponderous across the moon. He spoke also, of course, of the islanders, who climbed the palms to pick the coconuts and to drain the fermented sap for drink. Who dived into the blue water of the bay early in the morning to catch the fish that he ate for breakfast. Who sent the fruit bats wheeling and screaming out of their dark caves into the white of noon with their rifles. He had come across a little heap of black bodies on their backs in the sand, eyes blinking wearily, furred arms clenching and unclenching in their death throes, the cry from their pink throats silent to his ears. He was not sure who ate the fruit bats. None of this, perhaps, was what they wanted to know or what they wanted to hear. Perhaps they did not want, especially, to know what a nice place this was to be, but Jonathan told them anyway, filling pages with colours and sounds.

That afternoon, for some reason, the canoe came across from the mainland freighted with tourists, their thick brown suitcases piled at the bow, their sharp bright white trousers glimmering in the rear in the shade of the awning. Jonathan watched from the balcony of his beach hut as they landed, spreading themselves along the strand, calling the names of the cafes and huts to each other, while the islanders stood in the sea tossing suitcases lightly onto the shore. Later he watched them from the corner of the cafe; none of his brothers had come over on the boat as he had half-hoped, to give him their company, or to tell him where to go next, and he was the only person sitting alone at a table. But it was easy enough to throng the seats around him with his brothers' presence, to feel their comfort round him, and to stare out together at the rest. The tourists had come across in pairs, mainly, a few of them in larger groups, but within these couples could easily be distinguished; Jonathan understood that the atmosphere of this little island was such that one came to have sex here, to

27

relax and enjoy undiluted sensuality. He watched as the couples bent towards one another across the tables, sometimes murmuring, sometimes laughing sudden and loud as if to throw their pleasure out into the middle of the room for the consumption of any bystander.

As the evening went on they began to dance, swaying close together to mournful ballads played on a decayed guitar, moving so slowly that the paraffin lamps hardly flared as they passed. Jonathan noticed – it struck him now as it had not when the visitors climbed the beach that afternoon – how wide was the difference in size between the male and female halves of these partnerships. As they clung together in the throes of the dance the women seemed all but submerged beneath the width and height of the men. Jonathan wondered what this would feel like. He smiled, realizing that he had been composing a sentence home about how the tourists had unnatural habits. One of the couples had moved off the dance floor and was straying out into the open. He followed as they wandered down the narrow path between the coconut palms and onto the sand. He sat on a log to watch them, silhouetted clearly against the silvered sea as they walked towards the water, hand in hand. The man, taller and broader and blonder than Jonathan, must come from some distant northern country, though Jonathan was not long enough outside Lelaki to be able very accurately to distinguish between northern races. The woman, though, was from the Islands. Jonathan had heard her speaking the language, and now her small, dark, fragile body swayed gracefully down to the sea. He was not surprised to see them kiss, still outlined against the sea, to see the man's hands moving about on the woman's body. He could imagine, were his brothers with him, that they would likely lie together at the tide's edge; he shivered lightly at the thought of a brother's teeth caressing the angle of his collar bone, of how his tongue might run lightly down his body. He blinked and looked back at the beach, to where they were lying now, the man having lifted the woman off her feet and put her down on the sand, so that he loomed over her, casting a long shadow up the strand. It seemed to Jonathan that this was as much the mating of two different species as he could imagine, that small frail thing crushed beneath so much blond flesh.

He was unable to sleep that night, lying entombed behind the shutters that shut out all light along with the insects. The wind was rising. With the shutters open he could hear faint sounds still coming from the cafe, a vague murmur of enjoyment and swirls of laughter brought him on sudden gusts. Standing at the window watching the fronds of the coconut palms bending, Jonathan was reminded that one of the few specific warnings he had received concerned the danger of standing beneath a coconut palm in a high wind. He had an urge to go out at once and subject himself to the risk, face turned up to watch the deadly fruit hurtling down.

As the wind rose the sounds of laughter were becoming less distinct. Letting his mind rove out over the island, Jonathan imagined that the couple on the beach had been driven indoors by the sand whipping into their faces, that the island was almost swept clear of human form by the simple cleansing wind. As it rose, the beach huts themselves would lift abruptly in the air and, turning over and over like crumpled cardboard, roll down into the sea, where they would be spun out into the bay by the current. Until the island was a wild tangle of forest, and palms, and sand, on the beach a few bleached bones of wood jutting up into the sun. Jonathan lay on the bed feeling the rush of the wind under his hut, the faintest lift of the planking as it gusted.

The next morning the wind had stilled. Jonathan walked inland, away from the beach where the couples lay on their towels under the palms. The ground rose, an even hump of hill, between one side of the island and the other; the path over the hill was a wide shadeless track of beaten earth. People lifted themselves from rice fields to stare as he walked past; children ran to the doors of houses to look at him.

Jonathan pushed himself past them against the wall of their resistance; he wondered what could be hidden on the other shore where the tourist canoes did not dock, so easily and yet so completely hidden by the shadeless heat and the dusty uphill path.

He passed through a hamlet, huts loosely strung out along the track. A group of boys were standing over the water pump, and as he came towards them they giggled at one another and then fell silent abruptly, gazing at him. Perhaps I am the first they have seen, Jonathan thought, letting himself not try too hard to read their stares.

The path ended in a narrow cove. More coconut palms and the sea spread out before him again, quiet sand and the blue of the ocean. As he stood looking out, Jonathan heard a rustling behind him: the boys from the village had followed him, their feet fast and quiet on the dusty track. They were alone on the deserted beach. Feeling the sun beating on the top of his head, Jonathan walked out into the water. He looked to see whether the boys would come after him, but they had turned aside to sit on a log beneath the palms and seemed no longer to watch him, immersed in a game of their own. Without a mask the life under the water was vague; Jonathan found himself constructing sea snakes from tiny eels, the black spines of sea urchins from fragments waving on the sand, a suddenly hostile environment to his blurred vision. It seemed safer to lie on his back and feel the sun burn into his eyelids.

Out of the water, his shirt drying in the sand, Jonathan lay down again and prepared himself for the return journey in the height of the heat, trying to think with not too great an intensity of the cold drink that the other side of the island offered, the feel of ice under his tongue. He opened his eyes at the sound of shuffling feet; the boys were gathered round him, smiling now, pointing up into the palms and showing him their long curved knives.

"Drink," they said. "Good," and gesticulated at the coconuts high above his head. Jonathan smiled back. He watched as they selected one of the trees and the tallest of them climbed easily up, setting his feet into notches in the trunk. The boys below danced out of the way of the rain of falling coconuts, shrieking and calling. When they brought one to Jonathan, a hole neatly carved out of the top, they sat down near him and drank themselves, passing coconuts between them and eyeing him over the wide green spheres as they drank.

When he had finished Jonathan fished out what damp coins were in his pocket and handed them over. The boys nodded and got up in a body and disappeared up the path, laughing and nudging one another and giving him backward glances. Jonathan lay back in the shade and slept. When he woke he was wondering why the boys had hardly spoken to him; they surely must speak enough of his language to sell coconuts and beer to tourists every day. Perhaps he was dangerous to speak to, like the old witch of the fairy tale who lures you with ordinary domestic conversation until suddenly you are enslaved. His eyes still closed, Jonathan suddenly felt again another, deeper shade. For a moment he could not place it, could feel only the darkness of it, and the weight of the heat outside in the bright sunlight that enclosed him in this stillness. Then his mind provided the smell of browning grass and the shrieks of some game being played across the green. The dark summer shadow of the tree outside his father's house, that summer he had decided not to stay at school with his brothers and came back instead to see how his father was, and who he was. It was an odd time to choose, because he was only fourteen or so, the age when he most wanted to be with his brothers every moment of the day . And he had been lonely, lying under that tree longing for a brotherly touch. Yet he must have had some reason, something he thought he could find out from the dry, detached person his father turned out to be, elderly even then, having waited into his fifties for offspring. He remembered that they would look at one another across the table, smiling and looking, silent, and then he would go and lie splayed out under the dark green of the tree and feel the blood running in his veins and the ground, cool in that spot even in the heat of summer, still and flat and dry under him.

He turned his head and opened his eyes. One of the boys had come back, the tall one who had climbed the tree. He was sitting nearby, idly shredding the fibres of an old coconut husk into the sand. When he saw Jonathan move he looked across and smiled, a slow particular smile. Jonathan smiled back, unfocused. The boy laid the coconut husk carefully down in the sand in front of him, still holding Jonathan's gaze. Jonathan considered closing his eyes to shut out his stare, but only blinked.

At last the boy asked, clearly and slowly: "Do you want me?" Jonathan shook his head, as carefully as the boy had spoken, the slightest of movements. He reached out his hand to his shirt, still lying beside him in the sand.

"Good and cheap," the boy said, standing up, making a step towards him.

"No, thank you." Jonathan put the shirt over his head. It smelt of salt and heat.

"You want it. You like it." The boy paused, gathering words, his eyes steady and unmoving, "I know what you want. I do it." Jonathan sighed and shook his head again.

Finally the boy narrowed his eyes and shrugged. He turned up the track, "Fuck you."

As he trailed up the dusty path Jonathan kept his eyes on the beaten dirt a few feet ahead of him. The boys were clustered round the pump in the village as if they had never left; again they fell silent as he passed. The women in the rice fields, even the children at the doors of the huts, seemed to be in the same positions as they had that morning; they moved only to stare at him, unspeaking.

In his beach hut, Jonathan picked up his mask and snorkel. The sand of the beach burnt into the soles of his feet. He swam out to sea until the cries of tourists playing with beach balls in the shallows were silenced by distance, until the sand itself could no longer be seen and the island, as he looked back, treading water gently, was a hump of green rising out of the blue sea, ragged-edged with the fronds of palms. Then he turned over on his face and stared down into the darkened water.

It was not, surely, to discover that on the most beautiful of the Islands a tourist would be offered, patiently and as a matter of course, the bodies of the inhabitants, that he had been sent. Sitting under the canoe's heavy canvas awning, Jonathan kept his eyes on the mainland that drew towards them. Already he could make out the lines of beached canoes; soon the buses would come into view, their noses pointed toward the city. He had caught the market boat, and trussed pigs squeaked thinly at his feet. The gnarled women carrying their sacks to market reassured him a little, that there was some other economy here than the sale of flesh. Or perhaps it was that the young sold themselves and the old the produce of their land. As they neared the beach a young man leapt into the water to steer the prow of the canoe up the sand. He stood up to his knees taking bundles as their owners skipped over the side; but when Jonathan moved to the edge of the boat he found himself grasped under the armpits and lifted like a small child to the safety of dry land. The intimacy of the gesture wrapped itself around him as he staggered through the soft sand to the line of buses.

Jonathan swayed as the bus shuddered along the weaving, dusty road. He felt the print of strong hands cupping his chest. He felt marked, placed; that was all that tourists came looking for, and he was no different. Everyone knew that the Lelaki, having only each other, used each other for sex; that was how, he knew, people explained his preference to themselves. It was a question of circumstances, faintly disgusting even to a tolerant people used to accommodating the whims of conquering strangers, but not something for which they would be so uncivilized as to blame him personally. To them he was the result of a benighting accident, not the product of a reasoned and considered choice; and anyway he represented an opportunity, another means to survival. He was only a different variety of tourist, one that required a slight revision in the commercial arrangements, one who would want thin, lithe young boys with dark, innocent eyes, instead of the dark, lithe girls that the rest of them, mostly, wanted. It was not, it seemed, so unlikely a matter in itself, the taste that foreigners exhibited for little boys. The Islanders were used to tall blond men from cold places who wanted dark, hot, fresh boys, and who would pay for them. Jonathan watched the dust roll out behind the bus, coating the banana trees by the roadside. He felt the press of hands around his chest. As if he, like the men from wherever else, could want something, somebody, so different, so much not himself.

Chapter 2

The fountain appeared to cascade from the ceiling and, reaching the marbled floor of the lobby, to leap back up toward the roof, glittering and sparkling with eagerness. On the first floor balcony a three-piece band played dance tunes, the cellist's notes wafting between the splashings of the fountain. The waiter taking Jonathan's order, offering a selection of cakes and discussing the merits of teas, wore tails. Those who brought plates to the table or whisked away his crumbs wore less formal dress, subtle distinctions within a minutely articulated hierarchy.

Jonathan luxuriated, waiting, deep in his chair. He was vague as to the departed civilization that the hotel sought to recreate; the Islands had had so many conquerors, in such quick succession, and this baroque excess of formality could have come from any of them. Even perhaps his own, not the less so for his feeling of amusement and strangeness at the glittering spectacle. He waited: he would feel them coming, some sense they all had but had not bothered to name would flower a recognition in his brain as they came close. Long before he saw them his whole body would be alert to their presence. Almost he had it now, that antecedent knowledge, in his eagerness for the brothers' arrival. He forked a last fragment of tart into his mouth and felt, as the succulence hit his taste buds, that shift and opening in his mind that meant they were here.

"I don't understand this country. And neither do any of you." They laughed and raised their glasses. It was too soon; they could not be expected to understand anything, yet. They needed to acclimatize. As one or other put down his glass it was immediately replenished. Thin black and white clad figures moved quietly round them, weaving in and out.

Someone gestured at the waiters' self-deprecating dance, "They seem to understand us."

"On more than a commercial level, you mean. Beyond assuming that we desire to drink."

"It could be that they desire us to drink, and we're simply going along with it."

"Are we so suggestible?"

"Of course we are. That's always been the point."

"Not from outside. Not externally suggestible."

"I don't know if our psyche could tell the difference."

They disputed mainly for the sake of a familiar noise, for the pleasure of hearing themselves speak. They had not realized that one of the consequences of separation would be a new isolation of their own individual voice, that it would sound naked, altered somehow by solitude. And so they talked for the intermingling of familiar tones, the rising and falling and blending of a dozen similar voices; it was a way of remembering who they were, finding something they had not quite known had been lost.

"How do they see us?"

They looked round. The tables were scattered at discreet intervals about the high echoing space. Others taking their early evening drinks were distant, sipping at glasses in contemplation of the fountain, in perusal of some guidebook. Tourists and locals alike took no account of the distinguishing characteristics of this particular group; they were merely a group of representatives of a former colonial power making, as one might expect, somewhat too much noise over their pleasure.

"They've assimilated us."

"How can we know how they see us until we can see them?" The brothers laughed, having allowed themselves to drink rather more than usual.

"They've got a whirlpool bath here," Jonathan said. "D'you think we're that assimilated?" They giggled.

* * *

He pushed the pack of cigarettes across the table at Jonathan. An old Lelaki brand name, though no one at home had smoked for generations.

"I think it's been bred out of us," Jonathan said, shaking his head. He watched the words pass across the stranger's mind, finding no point of entry.

Tomas shrugged, spilling the remark finally onto the tiled floor to be lost unnoticed underfoot. He opened the carton neatly with one hand and brought a cigarette to his lips.

"You know what they say? That a man who doesn't smoke in this country is a revolutionary." Smoke curled out of his mouth as he grinned. "The communists teach you a new way of life, you see. No drink, no cigarettes, no vices. No sex."

Their table was thrust up against an expanse of plate glass. Jonathan thought he recognised the style of home, meticulously achieved some fifty years after the vogue had passed. Across the road groups of girls were returning to school after lunch. Their uniforms, navy blue pinafores, blouses of fluorescent whiteness, the painted neatness of their hair, added to Jonathan's sense of temporal dislocation. The Islands had acquired and retained a religion from an earlier colonizer; that obedient file preserved perfectly the forms of a culture that elsewhere must have been superceded long since.

"Isn't that what the Church has been saying all along?" He watched as the iron gates of the school were swung shut. It seemed to him that the nun met his eyes as she let the latch fall into place.

"That is only what makes the new way so easy for us to accept. No," Tomas paused, inhaling deeply, "the new man is doing it for himself, and for the greater good of his people. Not for the good of his soul, to avoid sin." He examined his hands carefully, turning them over and spreading and closing his fingers, "The communists have a much better argument behind their prohibitions."

"I don't see it. Why can't you have a revolution and have more fun as a result? Wouldn't that go down even better with the man in the street?"

Tomas picked up the cigarette pack again and shook it gently before Jonathan's eyes, "It is no good you saying 'you' like that. I told you, I myself am not of this persuasion." He let the packet fall onto the shiny table top, "Though I have my sympathies. Do you realize that many of those girls, those nice respectable girls in their school uniforms – " They both turned to look at the solid grey building squatting in the heat across the road, "will have to sell themselves to stay at school and finish their courses? Not very often, of course, maybe once a term or so, to buy the books they can't do without."

The waitress put an avocado flip, gleaming in its green glass, down at Jonathan's elbow. Tomas sipped his coffee as Jonathan looked down into its green depths, "You see? You are an extravagant people. You think that indulgence is the answer, and that is what you have led us too to believe. More fun, more sex, more money, and all our troubles will be at an end – "

"Not anymore," Jonathan protested, "We're quite restrained ourselves these days. Did you know, the sticker on the President's desk last year used to say 'Nurturing, Conservation, Restraint.' "

"On your president's desk?"

"Yes."

Tomas returned his coffee cup to the precise centre of its saucer, "And this year? What does it say this year?" He smiled winningly, as if extracting a confession from a reluctant child.

"The same sort of thing, obviously."

"It is not obvious to me at all. Your whole civilization is built on expansion, global consumerism. You spread yourselves out, gobbling up little pieces of land here, minerals there, now fishing rights, now some supposedly strategic port – and you wish me to believe that this has changed because you have become – just because you think you can control everything, even evolution – a nation of nice queer blond boys?"

Tomas fumbled for another cigarette. Jonathan spooned avocado sludge into his mouth with a rhythmic movement. Tomas held his lighter clenched in his fist for a moment before snapping it shut and putting it on the table in front of him.

"Now, I know what your president means, all those three words to him, they really mean 'Consolidate.' That, I can understand. You want to be sure of what you have before you go on to grab some more, you are not so reckless as you once were. But, it makes no difference. Underneath you are the same." He was watching the school building again, scanning each window minutely as if he were able to look through the wall into the classrooms at the blue-clad girls at their secret lessons. "This country has had enough of your message. We need a new way to live."

"I'm not sure that being a smoker is much of a disguise."

Tomas gestured impatiently, "I have told you, I'm not a communist. But it is coming, and there is nothing you can do now to stop it. Tell that to your president. Maybe he will put it on his new sticker."

Jonathan watched him walk quickly away down the street, heels striking the pavement sharply as if in reproof. He would, he realized, have to admit in his report that he could not say whether he had approached Tomas or Tomas him. But he was left with a clear sense of having had something – even if he did not know exactly what – laid very deliberately in front of him. The second avocado flip stood half-finished on the table.

"Restraint." He stood and pushed it away from him.

He walked desultorily through the streets. There were parks in this part of the city, but they were flat and treeless and lacked the shade he sought. His shirt had begun to attach itself to his body. After half-an-hour he found himself outside his embassy, arrived there without conscious intent. A Lelaki guard stood outside, leaning against the gates, his machine gun propped against the stone gatepost. In front of the entrance two squat, heavy-leaved trees reared out of the pavement. Jonathan paused beneath one, reaching out to touch the thick trunk, its surface faintly damp beneath his fingers.

When he looked up the guard was standing just outside the circle of shade, hands in his pockets. "I wouldn't stand there, brother, if I were you." As he spoke he took another step backwards, "The locals say those trees are full of evil spirits. Make you ill if you stand under there without their permission."

Jonathan withdrew his hands from the trunk and looked up at the dark, limp foliage, "So what did we plant them for?"

The guard grinned and turned back to his post at the gates, "We weren't about to take any notice of what they said, were we."

Jonathan stood irresolute, the trees at his back and the solid white mansion before him, swept paving stones leading to the portico. It had a faint look of neglect, of departed splendour, perhaps even of unease.

"Keeps the demonstrations away, anyway. Nobody'll stand outside here at night." The guard cocked his head to one side, letting a lock of hair fall across his eyes: "Homesick? Go in and read the papers," he flicked the hair back, "have a cup of coffee. It's as good as being there. Air-conditioned, too."

"How come they don't make you sick, these trees?"

"Used to. Then I had a little talk with them, came to an understanding." He leaned his head back against the gate.

Jonathan walked on. The road led to the sea, lying flat and metallic in the thick afternoon heat behind a low concrete retaining wall. Jonathan sat, remembering that the sunset was said to be spectacular here. At the moment the haze of afternoon light revealed only the dim shapes of a few military vessels anchored beyond the harbour. Perhaps the setting sun reflected to advantage off the thin slick of oil in the bay. He glanced down, to see that sweat had soaked the waistband of his trousers and was welling up his shirt front.

On the way back to his hotel he turned in at the door of a bar, one of a dozen in the street, their neon lights flashing pallidly in the sunlight. The air conditioning reached out, icing the shirt to his back at once.

The waiter put his beer down on a little mat and paused, leaning slightly on the table, his hip jutting through the thin black of his trousers. "Something else?" His hand waved faintly towards the back of the bar. The girls were sitting at the end of the empty counter, legs curled round the high stools, elbows on the formica, talking amongst themselves, waiting for the arrival of evening and customers. "No boys, I'm sorry."

"Could I talk to one of your girls? For money?" The waiter's face said nothing. He shrugged. Jonathan watched him walk down the bar. As he talked the girls twisted round on their stools to look him over, then turned away to whisper to one another, glancing back over their shoulders quickly, as if they were afraid he might have moved towards them in the moment of their inattention. Finally one of them slid to the floor and came to his table, smoothing her fragment of skirt as she walked. She sat opposite him, smiling slightly at the table top, her hands folded in her lap.

"I'm just interested – in how things work," he said. She shifted slightly, moving back on the bench a little. As if he might be about to ask to see her health certificate. Jonathan studied the details of her make-up with the air of someone who expected that these minutiae would tell him what it could be like to be inside such a body. He had mastered the economics of the Islands and understood, therefore, that the government depended largely on tourism for foreign currency. And that the greater and more profitable part of that tourism concerned the sale of sex to foreign males and the sale of women complete, also, as brides. This latter practice seemed to Jonathan, as to his brothers, an astonishing barbarism, given the participating countries' professed belief in human rights. It seemed to him that the voluntary exile of the Baba-i, routinely still said to put the Lelaki beyond the pale in such matters, was as nothing in comparison to the sale of women into marital slavery.

But prostitution was an economic opportunity at

least, insecure and exploited no doubt, but not inhuman as slavery was inhuman. It was the Lelaki position, the one that the expedition trainers expounded, anyway, and Jonathan had found it persuasive and appropriately non-judgemental. Of course, he had expected to find the Island prostitutes slightly disturbing, as professional purveyors of a kind of sexual experience that instinctively, if not intellectually, he felt to be unnatural and faintly bestial. But he had not expected to feel revulsion for the work they must do. Sitting across the table from this small, carefully painted and manicured woman in her flimsy, revealing garments, the image of the huge blond man towering on the sand kept recurring to his mind.

"Do you get lots of customers?"

"Oh, they like me, I'm popular." She picked at the polish on her tapering fingernails. "It's not a busy time of day now. They like to come late at night." She gave him a knowing smile, as if forgetting for a second that she didn't have to make him want her.

"What would you do if you didn't work here?"

"Why you want to know?"

Jonathan lifted his hands vaguely, trying to look harmless, "I just wondered."

"Funny people, you are. Didn't think I'd see a Lelaki boy in here." She laughed, finding out something about this dangerous and ungodly people, "I guess you're filthy curious, like everybody else."

She sipped cautiously at her lemonade, "Work in another bar. That's the work there is."

"But do you like it?" She looked at him. He must be very stupid.

The door was pushed open and a dark shape propped itself up against the bar; it grunted familiarly at the waiter, loosening its collar and sighing, the noise a large quadruped, panda or polar bear, makes as it sits on its rump.

"It's not so bad. My family don't like it, but they like the money."

The polar bear had turned into a local businessman, stopping for a drink on his way home. He was talking to the waiter, glancing sideways at Jonathan's table. Then the waiter was leaning over Jonathan, "You will have to pay a little more, I think, if you wish more conversation. The girls will be very busy soon."

Jonathan looked outside; it would be cooler now that the sun was setting. He drained his glass and stood up. He pushed an extra note across the table.

She nodded, "I support my family, because of me they eat." In a moment she had been reabsorbed into the group of women who chatted on, leaning against the bar. As Jonathan emerged into the night a taxi slowed hopefully. He scrambled into it and watched the brightening lights flicker out across the pavement, wavering before his eyes with the speed of their passage through the city.

Chapter 3

His window looked down over the basketball pitch. Below him now a group of young men weaved and sprang, jostled one another and called in a frenzy of lunchtime idleness. He had wasted countless hours on that same court himself, weaving and yelling. The double panes of his window bleached out sound so that the mouths below opened and shut noiselessly, the clang and rattle of ball against post were gone; the game was as if played in pantomime. Were he to take the lift down to the ground floor, walk outside and stand by the edge of the court, watch the boys whirl past him, hear their laughter, their urgent signals, smell their sweat as they pranced, then Luke knew he would be overtaken by a powerful nostalgia. In a moment he would be filled with yearning for the days when he and his brothers, in their turn, had danced so on the asphalt, the old adrenalin would run again through his veins, and he would be leaning across the pitch, almost mixing with the players, screaming, "Pass, pass!" Luke remained where he was, hands in his pockets, staring down at the muted pageant laid out for his inspection.

From this distance it was as though he were compiling a computer analysis of the game. He ceased to watch the players, ceased also to feel the game through them as a pattern of expectations, possibilities, disappointments, near-misses. He saw instead a small ball bounced up and down, this way and that, flung at a net, ricocheting away. He saw a number of players fighting for control over that ball, losing and regaining it; he saw how frequently the ball was beyond them, lost. What Luke saw, in fact, was how often the players missed their target, whether each other or the net. They were not, when it came to it, very good at basketball. Luke looked down over the younger generation, playing their national game with seemingly careless ineptitude.

It was recorded that the first time a Lelaki team had been beaten by a foreign side people had been mildly surprised but not especially concerned. They pointed to years of isolation from new developments in the game, to the unfamiliarity of our boys with competition on an international level. The blurred, flickering tape of that game was still available. What seemed so obviously revealed, to Luke's eye, had passed without notice or comment then; or perhaps they had seen and been unable to see, so shocking, unthinkable, was it. Playing a race that traditionally the Lelaki had always thought of as diminutive in comparison to themselves, on court the Lelaki team had been overshadowed by tall, agile, skeletal figures that wove effortlessly between, around, over them. Beneath him Luke watched the boys pant to a halt in the middle of the court, leaning together. Soon they began to leak away in twos and threes towards the changing rooms. In a few minutes they would be back in their suits and banging cheerfully into their offices, slightly red in the face, grinning, and convinced they had done themselves good. Luke looked sourly at the tops of their tousled blond heads. It seemed to him an incredible oversight that no one should have thought about the demands of basketball when selecting master Lelaki junior, super de luxe model. Did none, not one of those founding scientists, play the game or even follow it? Perhaps they thought the gradual increase in height, born of a superior diet and environment, would be enough. And of course they had added a few inches over the years, but a few inches added to an average height was no defence against the vast variations that female births will produce. If the Lelaki were never pygmies, they were not giants either; they might as well be pygmies, for all the difference it would make to Lelaki basketball standing in the world they had so triumphantly reentered. Of course any Lelaki was taller than the average product of any other country, but the point remained that he was not as tall as their basketball players.

Luke turned away from the empty court. The desk across the room was spread with papers, lying in wait. He was well aware that extremes of height were undesirable for any number of physiological reasons, but it seemed to him that a more satisfactory solution should have been found than simply to abandon basketball as if it were a necessary sacrifice to the cause of perfection and progress. To his mind, perfection necessarily included the capacity to play fluid, graceful, accurate and successful basketball, for which you needed elongated thigh bones.

The desk lay in wait. Luke crossed to it, sat down and pressed the intercom, keeping his gaze averted from the reports he had scattered across its surface.

"Tommy, a flask of coffee. Good game, I suppose?"

"Great." Still panting lightly.

"It was lousy as usual."

He must have put the coffee on as soon as he got in, for Luke had hardly time to raise his eyes to the ceiling and lean back in his chair before Tommy was through the door, the tray balanced neatly on outspread fingers.

"I watched you. All of you, you can't shoot to save yourselves."

"I know, you always do." Tommy poured two cups, still holding the tray on the fingertips of one hand, and put the flask and one cup down at Luke's elbow.

"Should've been a waiter."

"I was, in college." Tommy slid the tray under his arm and turned to the window, his own cup in the other hand.

Luke watched his profile, the heat of his recent exercise still flaring at his cheekbones. "Will you wait on me?"

He slid out from behind the desk to stand next to Tommy, his hand snaking quietly under his jacket, passing gently across his ribs, over his spine, coming to rest with Tommy's body held within his arm. Tommy kept his eyes on the ground below them.

"You're an aberration, you are," he said.

"Aren't we all." Luke let his hand fall.

"I wish you wouldn't watch me, playing. You make me drop things."

"I'm not, watching you. I'm watching the game — all of you."

Tommy turned his back to the window, moving himself out of range. "Solipsist. Voyeur." He left the room, the tray once more balanced and held aloft. Luke sighed, sitting at his desk. The reports awaited him.

It was as if, reading them, he were being shown a scene through thick, distorting glass. Where his own double glazing drained the world of sound but left actions clear to speak to him, this was bulging, unpredictable, now letting fragments of speech out toward him, now massing so that all he could make out was the vaguest blur. Luke put down the last report amidst the scatter. Then he began to tidy his desk, shuffling papers, bending back creased corners, until the reports were lined up in front of him, side by side like cards in an enormous game of patience. The agent's name appeared, precisely centered, in the middle of each first page. The address of their current Island station was ranged right, his own name and office ranged left. All perfectly, conventionally, laid out, an impressive demonstration of word processing skills. Checking their identifying codes, Luke noticed once again that they were all this year's crop, fresh from cadet school. A dozen neatly spaced reports on the situation in the Islands, entirely lucid but entirely opaque where they should have been illuminating. Perhaps there had been a failure in this year's training, or a radiation leak into the dormitories, affecting those parts of the brain responsible for interpretation of outside stimuli. No, they would all have been on field trips, passed tests, produced dummy reports. Someone would have noticed.

He pulled the nearest report back towards him: was it perhaps style, had some would-be creative artist slipped into the teaching staff, taught them all to report by suggestion and allusion? He read for the third time an account of a clandestine political meeting to which the agent had gained access by sufficiently disguising himself as to pass for a sympathetic foreigner from some other, neutral country. It might have been a dangerous thing to do; it had obviously required considerable preparation. And yet the report of events at this meeting amounted to nothing, to no more than a list of the topics on the agenda. The writer went into great detail about the clothing of those present, the weather that day, even the view he had from his seat of a banana tree outside the window. From his description, Luke could picture the scene clearly enough: the thin, wobbly table, the low hurried voices, the way they paused and looked towards the door at every unexpected sound. The agent was describing conspirators, after all, and such scenes are easy enough to imagine, whatever the setting. But however often he read it, he could get no hint of the flavour of that meeting, of their mood. The words on the page could as well cover the desperate last bickerings of a lost cause as they could a revolution that was about to set the country – the whole continent, maybe – alight end to end.

Luke leaned over and yelled into the intercom, "More coffee!"

He had to wait longer this time before the door from the outer office opened. Tommy slammed the tray down on the desk in front of him: "You have to be so rude?"

Luke stretched in his chair, "Sorry. I'm merely taking out the day's frustrations on you. It is more or less part of the job description, bearing the brunt of your superior's stress."

"You could go down to the whirlpool and tell a brother or two about it."

"Wouldn't that be cozy. No doubt if they thought this could be done by a team, they'd have put a few friendly faces in the office with me to start with."

"I don't see why my brother is more of a security risk than I am myself."

"Tommy, you're sweet. A model young man – and

that's saying something here amongst all us models, is it not."

Tommy reached over the desk and straightened one of the little piles, "Do I get a bonus if you take out too much on me?"

"I suppose you've read these reports?" Tommy nodded. "What do they tell you?"

Tommy smiled, "It's like being there. All those places, and the people, women and children, and little huts on stilts."

"A travelogue, you mean."

"Don't you feel it? It's like reading poetry."

Luke poured coffee into his cup, "And what does this poetry tell you about the political situation?"

Tommy frowned, looking at the neat row of papers on the desk. "It doesn't give you the detail, more of an atmosphere."

"And I am supposed to base my recommendations on a poetic atmosphere."

"Well, can't you send someone else? Get more reports? I could go – "

"And send me back more poetry. I don't think I see the usefulness of more reports."

"But isn't this place supposed to be the next candidate for the big experiment? Our friendly ally the new super race, third world style."

Luke examined the depths of his cup, "And who told you that?"

Tommy was leaning against the window, his legs crossed at the ankle, the pose of ease and confidence. "It's more or less in your job description. Find a nice ex-colony, not too backward, reliably dependent on us for economic survival, and offer them the ultimate Lelaki aid."

"And why would we want to do that?"

Tommy grinned, shrugged, "I reckon the President's lonely, he's tired of being the bogeyman of the universe."

"If you want to get on in this new thrusting diplomatic of ours, Tommy, never suggest that policy is in any way influenced by the President's human frailties."

"No, sir. And never suggest that the only reason for not having a coffee machine is to give you an excuse to bully me."

"Oh, that's obvious." Luke felt unexpectedly cheerful as if somewhere recently light had been shed on his problem, "It's to teach you to be suitably subordinate."

Luke stood, looking down on the basketball court. It lay quiet in the evening air, abandoned even by the crowd who liked to hang about after work, to lean against the wire fencing and watch one another drawing dull clangs from the iron hoop dug into the wall. Tommy and his brothers, they were down in the bars now, or at their relaxation classes, or at home playing multi-terminal video games. Preparing themselves for their future when they would be middle-aged corporate successes just like their fathers. Luke wondered whether his own faint unease, a sense of not fitting absolutely into the comfortable niche prepared for his use, did not stem from his having departed from the family profession in order to savour the new challenge of the diplomatic. Perhaps he didn't have it in him. The official line continued to be that the capacity for change and innovation was provided for by subtle new gene combinations. Technically, it was explained, the possible permutations were far more numerous, uncountably more numerous than those available to people using natural means of variation. In terms of mental equipment he ought, Luke was aware, to be perfectly capable of the leaps of imagination required to understand and communicate with other cultures. It was not, he suspected, any individual failing of his own that was really the cause of his problem. Rather it was that in doing, or trying to do these things, he was necessarily doing something that the Lelaki had not done for generations. Surely it was not surprising if he felt odd, apart even from his closest brothers, as if he saw their well-ordered world from a slightly skewed perspective. Not surprising if he couldn't consistently do it – see that other place clear – at all.

The reports were still piled in the centre of his desk. Luke had no further need to read them; he could have walked through the building chanting them line by line, he had by now read them so many times. So there was nothing tieing him to the office, he could as well go home and think about them there. There would be someone at home he could rouse up to talk to, have a late night game of chess with. Even if they were all asleep, it would be soothing to lie on his bed knowing that others were all round him, quiet and peaceful, a wall away in any direction. Or it ought to be soothing; yet, without quite knowing why, he went on standing by the window, looking down on silent asphalt. As if understanding might be present somewhere in the room, could he only surprise it, catch it unexpectedly out the corner of his eye. Luke leaned his head on the glass. As if it were truth he was after, as if it were a revelation that he sought. When he knew no truth, and it would be of no use to him if he did. He needed to know what he should say. It was much more difficult.

The map hung dimly beside the bookcase. Luke walked over to his desk and turned it on. It flashed at once into brilliant colour, the relief springing out towards him, the oceans sinking into graduated blues. In the deep blue of the empty ocean the Islands, flung down in a mass, sparkled a charming yellow. It was a milder version of the brisk cheerful orange that Lelaki had recently adopted to signify itself, assertive and modern without threatening associations. Even a glance at the map reinforced the Islands' significance, the only handful of dry land between three vast landmasses. So important as a stepping stone, a lookout post, a first line of defence. Standing in front of the map, scrolling it so that the Islands stood at its centre, Luke was again surprised that no one else should have taken advantage of Lelaki passivity during their years of isolation to move into those little yellow jewels. Perhaps they thought that would be to risk tempting the Lelaki wolf from its lair. Perhaps they even thought that, provoked, they might release the offspring onto the world like a newly virulent

51

chemical weapon. It would never have happened, of course; even if there had been a way to impose the Lelaki technology, it would have been a suicidal move. Defence of their old-fashioned biology was surely the only issue guaranteed to unite the rest of the world against a common foe.

Those huge landmasses squatting round the ocean. But they were not as unified as they looked; that cohesion was an effect of the eye, seeing choice in juxtaposition, bonds in boundary lines. Those borders etched across the map were sores, in truth, barely-healed scabs at best. The thing to do was to pick them off one by one; persuade them one at a time, play them off against each other, search out their individual fears.

It was unfortunate that Tommy had leapt to the conclusion that the Islands were first in line for treatment, unfortunate that he had realized so readily that treatment was what was under consideration. The news might spread anywhere, for all their isolation. It would take very little to start a scare globally and bring a mob of zealots down on them: the bogeyman is coming to kill your women and turn your sons into fairy robots. And meanwhile he did not know what was going on in the Islands. Luke turned back to his desk. In the silence he could hear the faint metallic whine of the garbage machine as it wheezed past in the street below, pick-up arms clattering faintly in the wind of its own passage.

Chapter 4

Luke never knew quite how he wrote the recommendations that, together with his synthesis and glosses of the agents' reports, wound their way, with appropriate security, up the hierarchy until they arrived, much pencilled over but in essence his own, in the President's hands. In his lighter moments, prone and sweating in the sauna, careless of everything, he would say that he made it up, the whole thing, out of whole cloth. Giving a lecture at the staff college, an old hand dishing out the tricks of the trade to eager neophytes, he would pass out abbreviated copies as an example of the necessity for a diplomat to extrapolate fearlessly from the facts at his disposal. Privately, Luke tried not think about it too frequently – it was too vertiginous – and when he did, told himself that he had never been, before or since, so creative. And if those agents had not been so vague, so deliberately vague, he would not have had so much to wing it. He had been covering up their failure, their collective seduction by the sirens of the Islands. The best of it was that, once acted upon, it was impossible any longer to assess whether his report had in fact been based on accurate information or sound speculation. The more Luke used it as an example of excellence for his students, the more it assumed the unquestionable status of gospel. It became true because he had made it so.

The Situation in the Islands

All sources, official and unofficial, agree that an economic crisis is imminent. In large part, this has been brought about by the collapse of prices for traditional Island exports – sugar, bananas, coconut-based products – in the world market. The profitability of these commodities has been reduced globally, sugar having been the most severely affected by fluctuations in world demand and a sustained long term decrease in price due to over-production. Sugar is by a considerable margin the chief Island cash crop. The impact on the Islands has been especially marked, furthermore, since producers have made few attempts to adapt to changes in economic conditions. Where modernization has taken place, and productivity increased and costs reduced as a result, the benefit has not been ploughed back into the industry or into diversification of the economic base.

The owners of the sugar plantations (locally known, not inaccurately, as 'barons') have been accustomed for some generations to a very high rate of return on their land. Sugar production and their entry into the market began at a time when this particular commodity was at a premium. The initial high price was subsequently artificially maintained by a Lelaki subsidy. It may be recalled that our continuing to buy at an inflated guaranteed rate was the only condition imposed when the Islands negotiated their colonial status, the local government of the time being comprised of the barons and their representatives. This arrangement remained in place, of course, through the years of isolation, since the Islands had nothing to gain by reneging on an agreement that, in the absence of our military from the Island bases, required nothing from them. Conditioned, perhaps, by years of prosperity and predictable profits, the barons were slow to accept the need to modernize in order to compete with other producers; the withdrawal of our guaranteed price did produce some attempts at reorganization, but even those owners who reorganized assumed that doing so would enable them to retain the profit levels available to them under the colonial system. They continued to appropriate profits for personal use, therefore, rather than diverting funds for improvements or for maintaining the fertility of the land.

Meanwhile, prices have continued to fall, and are

reaching a level so low that it will soon not be economic for the Island landowners to produce at all on their neglected, overused land. Already some thirty per cent of the land has been left to lie fallow, and the indications are that this figure will rise steeply over the next few years. There has been some switching between crops, away from sugar into those whose prices have held up marginally better. But this is having relatively little impact, since commodity prices continue to fall generally, and since the barons are reluctant to make costly experiments, preferring to wait out the slump in hopes that the price of sugar will eventually rise. Such land as has been used for alternative crops has been used for those requiring less labour-intensive modes of production (the coconut being given preference over the pineapple, despite the latter's higher price in the market, because pineapples require constant attention while coconuts grow of themselves) – so agricultural workers have obtained little benefit from those few changes that have been made.

The life of the sugar workers has always been marginal. The cyclical nature of the crop requires that they work in the field for no more than six months of the year, during planting and harvest. The wages earned in these periods of activity are expected to sustain them through the remainder of the year. The barons naturally own not only the cultivated fields but also the land on which the workers build their houses, and do not allow that any of their fertile soil should be wasted by workers growing food crops for their own consumption. This continues to be the case even where a landowner has decided that, in the current economic circumstances, it is not worth his while to plant his land for the coming year. There is strong resistance to the idea of leasing or lending land in case he should think of something better to do with it, or some new crop come to seem profitable due to a change in the world market. The economic and social structures, equally, are built upon the workers' dependence on the landowners, rather than on the land, for survival. Control of the land is essential to the barons' way of life and sense of identity; they feel very intensely that a self-sufficient peasantry is a dangerous one.

Government in the Islands is totalitarian, although opposition parties are theoretically free to operate. The next election is due in two years' time; it is expected that the existing incumbent will retain power – he has a large measure of popular support, and it is generally felt to be both futile and dangerous to present an alternative programme to the people. The inhabitants of the Islands are prepared to tolerate a high degree of control in the interests of stability; it is, of course, this stability that the regime presents itself as offering. Backed by an obedient bureaucracy and a strong military, the president is able to provide a satisfactory degree of efficiency in the running of the country, particularly in terms of the provision of law and order. The previous decades in the Islands have been, accordingly, peaceful and free from popular unrest. The resources of the government are, however, limited, firstly by the decline in the export trade and consequently in tax and tariff revenue, and secondly by the demands of the president's personal and family fortunes. These latter are large enough, treasury reports indicate, to represent a drain on the Island economy; this effect is exacerbated by the flight of presidential capital abroad.

The problem of limited resources has hitherto been solved by the president's passing on a certain percentage of the duties of law and order enforcement to his powerful allies among the landowners. In return for local power in their regions, much of the administration of peacekeeping has been turned over to the barons. This is in essence merely a continuation of the practice general in the Islands in colonial times, when barons retained their traditional power over the lives of the peasants who lived and worked on their land and over the administration of justice in the regions.

The president has made little attempt to adapt his policies to the widespread poverty and destitution that is appearing in the Islands in the wake of economic depression. There is no evidence of either welfare programmes or propaganda exercises; the government appears confident of the power of a continued appeal to tradition and traditional security. The sugar workers, in particular, have always been poor; the landowners have tended to assume that both the newly destitute and the increasingly impoverished will simply accept their deteriorating lot.

Unfortunately, this has proved a naive hope. With the new poverty has gradually come a new unrest. There have been increasing demands for land reform, as well as other means to a redistribution of wealth. There have also been claims that the Island economy is suffering due to the presence in the industrialized cities of Lelaki-owned businesses whose profits are enjoyed overseas. The agents' reports give no precise timings for the beginnings of what by now might be described as a revolutionary movement, but it is reasonable to assume that the trouble began during our period of absence from the Islands, when influence was not exerted either physically or in terms of economic participation. Whatever the exact origins of the organization, it is evident that the momentum of the movement has increased markedly over the last few years. Unrest has so far been successfully contained, largely through an increase in military activity throughout the Islands and by the introduction of more stringent anti-insurgency laws. The limitations on the president's resources have led to some of this work of the suppression of insurgency also being delegated to the landowners' private armies, with some loss of efficiency and consistency as a result. To some degree, this placing of military power in the hands of local landowners has been counter-productive; the inevitable abuses consequent upon such a system have tended to play into the hands of the opposition. The president has been fairly successful, however, in maintaining his personal prestige. Bearing in mind that his government is identified with order and the rule of law, it will be seen that any signs of anarchy or disruption can readily be assigned to the fault of those rebelling against the existing system. It should also be considered that the infrastructure of the

Islands is relatively unsophisticated by Lelaki standards, rendering communication between the two hundred-odd islands of the group erratic and sometimes impossible. Government control of the media, on the other hand, is efficient and its control of information outside a local area almost complete – many alleged abuses by the militia are therefore simply not reported. The people can accordingly be persuaded to continue support for the government in the belief that in so doing they are opting for stability and staving off chaos.

Despite the success of the containment to date, the strength of popular discontent should not be underestimated. In advocating land reform and thus economic independence for all, and in suffering detention, torture and summary execution in defence of these aims, the revolutionaries have at least the advantage of seeming very much, in the popular mind, to be on the right side – the side of the angels, as the local saying is. As the economic crisis deepens this appeal will inevitably become more substantial until their cause may come to seem the only one offering hope for the future to the average worker in fear for his livelihood and that of his family.

The social organization of the Islands is a complex and layered phenomenon. Superficially, the ways of the Islands, the local domestic organization and the gender values that are taught in its homes and schools, might appear very similar to those obtaining on Lelaki before the discovery of the new technology. This is what would be expected of a former colony that has remained largely dependent on Lelaki for its export trade. The Islands have experienced, however, serial occupations by a variety of different cultures, and have shown themselves remarkably retentive of traditions culled from these disparate sources. Notably, the original Lelaki colonization, being relatively belated, was not successful – such not being by then the strategic aim of our forefathers, naturally – in dislodging a form of religion imposed by an earlier power. This religion is still in place, and still wields institutional power. In common with many other colonized cultures, the Islands retain in addition traces of the structures of its pre-colonial, tribal past – a strand to the Island situation that is difficult to quantify but perhaps dangerous to neglect. Precise information about the nature of the oldest Island culture is hard to obtain, early settlers having made no consistent attempt to record or preserve it, and the Islanders themselves not then keeping written records. However, it seems from early commentators that within the loosely woven communities of a primitive, agriculture-based economy, Island women enjoyed a significant degree of power and status by virtue of their participation in religious rituals which, in turn, ensured their involvement in matters of public policy. This status has not been preserved within the familial structure that pertains today, modelled as it is upon what was once our own social organization. However, although outwardly superceded, and looked upon by progressive elements as archaic, it would seem from some of the agents' reports that a measure of the original primitive power is ascribed to, and has unofficially been retained by, the Island women.

Female expectations of participation in decisions within the family, and of economic independence in the workplace, present difficulties for the Island men. They must negotiate a conflict of ideas: while they are anxious on the one hand to preserve local traditions and to remain true to their heritage, they are conscious of the requirements and necessities of progress. A stronger male rôle is identified in the Islands with modernity, and with the dynamism necessary if the country is to emerge from the long shadow of colonization. In addition, the indigenous culture has a long tradition of separation by gender for the purposes of schooling, work and the passing of leisure time. Although marriage is arranged on the basis of mutual attraction, childless partners do not spend time alone together on a regular basis, preferring the company of their same sex family members, workmates or friends acquired at school. Children, however, while their care is a female responsibility, are considered interesting and valuable by both partners; fathers are usually

59

attentive and affectionate to their children from their earliest years, paying considerable attention even to girl infants until they reach the age of eight or nine, when the girls tend to become absorbed into an all-female network of friends and care-givers. The Island religion supports and sustains this structuring of social relations; its concern with the preservation of sexual purity leads to a way of life where the mixing of the sexes is discouraged.

It will be clear from a reading of the attached precis of the agents' reports that the overwhelming feeling among the ordinary people of the Islands at present is one of confusion. They are beginning to think that change, both economic and political, may be inevitable, as well as probably desirable, but they do not know in which direction they should move. It will be obvious that this is a time when outside influence may be crucial in pushing the Islanders towards one or other kind of social change. It is clear, too, that intervention from a number of sources other than Lelaki must be assumed to be a possibility. While the evidence from the reports is suggestive rather than definitive, there is a strong likelihood that such intervention has already taken place, although attempts to exert influence may as yet not have progressed beyond the clandestine.

In the absence of Lelaki participation in Island affairs, a gradual escalation of unrest must be anticipated. Even with assistance from the private militia, the government must soon reach a point where containment will cease to be fully effective. Even without weapons provided by external sources, the rebels have sufficient hardware, some purchased through legitimate outlets, some captured from the militia, to fight a punishing guerilla campaign. This conflict could readily escalate into a civil war. It may be imagined that such a war, once begun, would be long drawn out and extremely damaging in terms of both loss of life and loss of economic production. A continued policy of non-intervention would, in short, be likely to lead to further more deeply entrenched poverty in the Islands, in both the short and medium terms.

The outcome in the long term is necessarily uncertain. In the event of an eventual victory for the government – although it is difficult to see how the rebels could ever be entirely removed from the many hideouts offered by the Islands' forests and mountains and remote villages – the Islands would be left deeply in debt, without any immediate prospect of higher prices on the world food markets, and with an antiquated economic and political structure. The victory of the rebels, on the other hand, must remain something of an unknown quality, given the imprecision of their announced programmes for reform. However, the nature of the regime against which they are fighting, the radical demands made for redistribution of property, and the tendency of the organization's structure towards egalitarianism, would lead one to expect the attempt to set up a new society on some version of the revolutionary communist model. With this ideology would be linked, it can be assumed, a rejection of links with former colonial oppressors and presumably a correspondingly greater interest in forming new links with other powers seen as either more politically sympathetic to the rebels or simply as common enemies of the old imperialists. In the event of a rebel-led victory, the retention of a Lelaki foothold in the region seems a forlorn and pious hope.

Should Lelaki intervention be thought an appropriate option, various possible forms for such intervention will need to be considered. It may be that a return to arrangements pertaining in colonial times would be sufficient to reduce poverty in the Islands and stabilize the present government. Such action might take the form of commodity guarantees along the lines of the original fixing of the sugar price, perhaps with arrangements to enforce a broadening of the cash crop base. It must be expected, however, that intervention of this nature would be widely unpopular in the Islands, even with those not influenced by the rebels, since such a move would be seen as a return to colonial government; the effect of economic support might paradoxically be to increase, rather than to quiet, rebel sentiment. Financial aid in such a form, moreover, could be of only limited benefit to the Island economy in the long run, since a more far reaching restructuring will be required to divert money into commercial and industrial development and into the urbanization necessary to support such changes.

The case for sending military aid to the president is in some ways compelling: the government is stable and an ally of long standing; it is probably only a matter of time before the rebel forces are supplied with equipment, if not personnel, by other powers interested in control over the Islands and the seas they command. However, a successful military intervention will leave the structural economic problems unsolved. Such aid would in practice need to be accompanied by financial aid and advice, and by a programme aimed at a restructuring of the economy. To send military reinforcements would, in effect, be to commit to a complete takeover of the Islands on a scale beyond that undertaken at the height of colonization. An additional factor to be taken into consideration when weighing such an intervention would be the difficulty of finalizing the conflict and achieving a complete victory over the rebels.

The advantages of an offer of the new technology, as compared to the previous options, lie in the indirectness of the intervention and in its limited nature. No large investment of either capital or manpower is required, and since the offer is on a voluntary level and can therefore be freely refused, Lelaki is less likely to be seen as attempting to impose its will by force in the tradition of imperialism. This in itself may increase the chances of such an offer's being accepted. The disadvantages attaching to this offer relate to the difficulties likely to be experienced in securing any such acceptance. The agents' reports suggest strategies – set out in detail below – for increasing the attractiveness of the technology to the Islanders. Consideration must also be given, however, to the likely reactions to the offer on the part of other nations. It will obviously be particularly important to avoid any hint of coercion. It might be desirable to ensure that the offer in fact takes the form of a request from the Island people, initiated and pursued by them in the first instance. The use of such a strategy might be sufficient to discourage a unified response from opponents of the new technology. While it would be unlikely to impress those most virulent against our way of life, an Island request could be enough to disarm some of the more liberal and neutral members of the international community.

In the light of the indications of the mood of the people given by the agents' reports, it would seem possible that the Islanders might be prepared to consider favourably an offer of the new technology, were such an offer made with appropriate sensitivity to local needs and conditions. It would appear that it would be unwise in the circumstances to suggest that offspring be available to the Islanders on the same terms as were applicable on Lelaki at the inception of the programme. It seems that it will be necessary to allow the Islanders to choose their own models, and that these models will be of both sexes. Given a racial mix that is not only varied but well-established and integrated on all levels of society, it may be that a choice of models within genders will be required. The Island stock is racially heterogeneous, and any attempt to synthesize this disparate heritage too quickly may be counterproductive. Since the Islands will be the first recipients of the technology outside Lelaki, they will of course be very wary of the experiment. It is crucial, therefore, that they be allowed to introduce a degree of their own variations, and that they should be seen, both by themselves and by the rest of the world, to be in control of the change to reproduction by offspring. It will be necessary, in other words, to allow the Islanders to depart significantly from the ideal of purity that offspring technology theoretically offers. It may be questioned whether the benefits gained will be sufficient to allow the Islanders fully to appreciate the potential of the technology, but it seems likely that after initial experimentation the selection of models would be likely to stabilize, leading to a gradual falling off in the variety of models. Whether this would in turn lead ultimately to a decline in the number of female offspring would depend on how closely the Island community came, with the benefit of the new technology, to mirror the Lelaki original. Our historical analyses and psychological studies both suggest that, once the new technology itself is accepted, the advantages of a single, unified specie are likely to become overwhelmingly persuasive.

Intersection

It was hard to watch the child off down the road. So light, so dark. So neat, the blue dress with the yellow sleeves, her hair lying dark and flat. Smiling, they ran off hand in hand, skipping as lightly as if nothing could ever come between them and safety, mother standing on the balcony, waiting. Ellie hardest of all to watch, running so bright and desperate, knowing that she has only this season left of school, maybe next if, somehow, money – her intelligence quick, unreproachful. Her mother's child, knowing necessity when she sees it. Carla marvels at herself, marvels. How this life is lived as if there were no other, as if it were the same as the old. Still the children must be sent off, their clothes clean as a wedding, shoes on their feet. Six times at least this morning she brushed the little one's hair. This is nothing, this is what we women of the Islands do. We send our children to school looking as if they might be the children of the baron himself, no less. It is our pride, maybe, and our way of saying, we know how much that education means. It is harder now, even than it used to be. The baron, maybe his little girl has a cupboard full of dresses. Ellie's dress is already a shade small. Again, soon, she will have to be looking about the village for a fragment that can't be passed on within a family. Or perhaps something will come from outside. Carla marvels at herself, her mind running on whether, perhaps, a bag of clothes might not come from the organization, and something in it that no one else needs more urgently than her Ellie. Wonders that she can think these things at all, when there is so much else.

If she were to get up, now, and walk through to the back. Automatically avoiding the gap in the flooring; though only a stranger would put their foot through it, not notice and risk landing under the house in the bare earth. Even those from the city, when the organization sent them, their feet were light and wary across the thinning floors. If she walked through, to the firepit and the chimney, the pans. All would be as usual, a string of half-dried mushrooms Ellie had picked in the fields the other day, half a bag of rice, and the cooking oil jar, empty. The cooking oil jar, empty. It was a small thing, but it spoke to her. She could see it quite clearly to herself, a pathetic thing on the shelf. The hub of the kitchen it ought to be, as it had been in her mother's kitchen, a big, greasy, generous thing, always being laced about in the pans, smoking over the flames, scenting the air rich. It was never empty, even in the off season, in her mother's kitchen as predictable as the heat in the cane fields.

Inside she can hear the kitten skittering across the ceiling joists, yowling. As thin as the rest of them. Even the pig, little black brute, eyes bright under the house, even the pig is thin. He will eat anything, anything. The kitten keeps its rickety legs out of his reach. Carla is accustomed to hunger; and the organization tries to make sure that they do not starve. Only when she and Victor were in charge of the distribution was there any danger of that, tending to leave themselves until last and finding it hard to keep enough back. Carla grinned, at how awkward it could be, to be so damn moral that you had to have someone else without quite all the scruples to save you from yourself.

They will be in school by now, in lessons, safely through the prayers and the patriotic songs that Ellie sings so dangerously, lately, disbelieving and as if she's making fun. And she too is safe enough here at home, waiting for it to be time to go to her neighbour's. The project to grow herbs for medicine is nothing new, they have discussed it twenty times over the months. If someone was going to start a rumour, that they were doing it for the men fighting in the

67

hills, they will have done it by now anyway. She isn't stupid enough to think that they don't know what goes on here, that there is no one in the village who speaks to the army. But even the government is in favour of herbal medicine these days. Let the people live off the land they haven't got. Keeps them out of the hospitals in town, where someone might notice them, might notice the malnutrition. Carla turns her head at a sudden sound beneath her; but it is only the pig turning and sighing under the house, digging his nose into the packed dirt and sighing.

She marvels at herself, that she can live with this fear. Victor, organizing across the valley. Talking urgently, quietly, in houses as bare as their own, floors as thin, jars as empty. Someone standing alert on the steps, for sounds of their coming. Victor going from house to house, faster as dark falls. It is so much easier to be out in the villages yourself, always moving, always talking; so much easier than to be sitting still on your own porch, waiting. So, it will be her turn again soon enough, and only the children must stay behind, sprawled together on her neighbour's floor. Still too young to be afraid to sleep, afraid of absences in the light of morning.

It is hard to remember the old life, hard to think back into it, although it is hardly more than a year since the organization came to the village. Once alive, you cannot imagine yourself unborn. She had been unconscious, a mere body, sunk in the cycle of changeless work. Always trying just to survive another season, another season. Praying that the owners would plant again, praying for prices to rise. Not praying, that she should be free of such bondage, not praying for life. Fear comes with life, with being alive. And now she is afraid. Carla looks at her bare toes stretching and curling on the floor in front of her. Every sinew of her body is at half-stretch, even now when she sits idle on this bench, her feet thrust out in front of her, her head leaning on her hand. The relaxation is the thinnest layer; at a single sound her limbs would stiffen, gather her, leap down the steps and weave her into the fields. She can feel the readiness, that terror, lying just beneath the surface, breathing softly.

It is odd, to be sitting on the porch, considering the manner of your death. How it will come. It is not sensible to think of it too often, of course, but sometimes to have looked and imagined, so that it will be no surprise, that can do no harm. It will be at night, for they always come at night when fear is easier to create and people are together in little clusters that will go down in a single burst from a machine gun if need be. The first thing they will see, those that are watching, are the lights flickering as they come up the tracks on the other side of the hill. Then they will be over the rise and the stabbing white lights of their trucks will be running down towards them. And behind the noise of their engines there will be the rustle of those leaving their houses by the back way, the sway of leaves as they rush into the fields. There should be enough time, it depends what they have come for. Perhaps someone has told, about her and Victor especially, and the trucks come directly. Perhaps she is alone that night and the little one is slow to wake, cries, will not go with Ellie to the neighbour's house. Perhaps she herself is asleep, wakes only with the spear of light through the shutter. Or perhaps she is up and away into the fields but not far enough, fast enough. They follow, they throw a ring round the village and drive her back until she is cornered on the track, the cane on either side and the moon streaming down.

Carla curls her toes. Then, if it is not too close to the village, they will rape her and shoot her, and perhaps leave a machine gun at her side to indicate that she was part of a guerilla ambush that they had to fight off. Or perhaps they will take her off some little way, rape her, strip her, leave her body in some half-dug grave across the valley. Or she will go back to their headquarters and they will torture her first for other names in the village, and then they will rape her, and strip her, and parcel her off by the roadside somewhere. There are more similarities than there are differences, and the end is always the same. No one lasts long, and sometimes Carla wonders that they can all bear it, looking round a room and knowing, that their time is so short. It will be worse, of course, when their people come down from the hills and the army is in the villages all the time, death every day. But at least then they will have weapons too, at least then it will be war and not terror.

* * *

Ellie tightens the link of Maria's arm in hers and extends her legs to leap over a dusty chasm in the road. Out of the corner of her eye she watches her sister dragging along just behind, singing to herself and swinging her schoolbag to and fro in front of her as she walks.

"You're going to drop that, Agñes."

Maria twists her head over her shoulder. Just now, her brothers are scurrying along peaceably enough, whispering. She turns back, "I'm going to be a film star." She will look like her cousin come back from the city on a visit, yellow hair, shiny stockings, shoes for inside as well as out.

"No you aren't." Ellie pokes her elbow gently into Maria's ribs, standing out through her pink blouse, "None of us aren't, going to be film stars."

"Could be. Anything's possible."

"Isn't."

"You don't have faith, Ellie." Maria straightens herself as she walks, imaging piety.

"Agñes, stop swinging your bag, you'll break the strap."

"It's heavy."

"Swinging it makes it heavier."

Agñes gives her bag a last swing, catching Ricky in the small of the back. The three brothers round on her: "Surprise attack! Retaliation raid: accka, accka, accka!"

Maria drags them apart, pushes Ricky up the road in front of her. Ellie walks on along the track backwards, watching: "Told you so, Agñes."

Maria takes her hand and they walk faster, leaving the little ones behind.

"That's what I'm going to be, a freedom fighter."

Maria grips her hand tighter, is almost pulling her along. They walk in silence. Ellie, breathless, gasps, "I am too, so."

"Stupid," Maria says, striding out, "Shut up, stupid."

71

Section 3: Items from Baba-i Library Records

It was the custom, once, to cite a people's creation myth as evidence of their former ways, or perhaps of a time when they saw the world as their own, unfiltered by the problematics of invasion or surrender. What these stories have in common is that the narrator's people are always the chosen one – the earth mother's favoured first born, or the refined result of a god's experimentation with the oven of creation, neither under nor over done. Only the Baba-i, alone among distinct races, have no comforting saga in which a genial creator places them centre stage, the rightful possessors of their place on earth. Certainly there are others who have been dispossessed from the lands of their birth and transported in slavery or rejection to struggle and die on inhospitable soil, and peoples whose origins are lost in the unrecorded violence of miscegenation. But only the Baba-i owe their existence entirely, and with a certainty that no myth can ameliorate, to human rather than divine agency.

* * *

Chapter 1

There is an old Baba-i joke about there being seventeen of them all together, and three of those are sheep. From the beginning they have always been very slow to allow any increase in their number, although at first this was seen as merely a response to the manifest limitations on the island capacity for food production and the consequent need to conserve scarce resources. Later, when huge floating fish farms had been set up off the southern shore, and, protected from their seal and bird predators, shoals spawned there in abundance, the Baba-i still showed no signs of raising the birth rate. The reasons were initially hardly conscious, simply a matter of unspoken consensus: they inchoately felt that the accident of their existence gave them no right to expand into deliberate community.

It is characteristic of the early history of the Baba-i that they made no decisions that they could avoid. So embittered was their view of the results of human action upon the world that they could only hope to achieve innocence through paralysis, by moving as little as they could upon the face of the earth. Necessarily, also, such actions as they did take tended to be reactive; they took the negative of the Lelaki position as their starting point. It was unavoidable that they choose who their children should be, however. For if they had attempted to remain true to some notion of purity by allowing no change in mothers' gene patterns, they would in effect have made a decision to reproduce themselves exactly. In the face of this inexorable truth, it was felt that change must be preferable. While a different nurture lay before the new offspring, almost unimaginably different from

75

that of their mothers, the Baba-i had seen too many Lelaki boys imaging their fathers' minds to feel safe in the assumption that a new environment alone could produce a child as other as that they felt they must construct if Baba-i was to escape the degeneracy they saw in Lelaki.

Predictably, then, the patterns that they chose for the reproduction of their offspring left much more to chance, or at least to the unknown effect of untried combinations, than would have been contemplated by the Lelaki – who would indeed have seen this methodology as an absurd and futile nonsense. The Baba-i professed a belief – if this is not too strong a term – in the value of chance, although the sources of this belief were as various as the ideological positions of the original population. For the women who found themselves together in that unpromising place had little in common besides the fact of their being inconveniently fertile. Those women who had arrived on Baba-i only after fighting an unsuccessful guerilla war against what they saw as a repressive and misogynist system identified chance with anarchy, as being somehow connected to the principle of freedom. There were those, on the other hand, who clung to the straw of chance as the last vestige of the natural law which man in his ungodly fashion had sought to wrench from its preordained path. If the Baba-i scientists also proclaimed variety as a positive quality, something that they would wish to see maximized, they in their turn justified this article of faith by the claim that homogeneity led to a belief in one's own national type as the norm for the world.

The children of the Baba-i were accordingly much more various in appearance, despite being very many fewer in number, than their male equivalents on Lelaki. If there was a trend discernible, it was towards a small, dark, rather hairy type. The Baba-i liked to make another joke about themselves to the effect that they were without conscious effort regressing toward the long-sought missing link.

It was high summer when the first meeting was held to consider the question of how their offspring should be reared. In those days the Baba-i were able to function only through an unwieldy form of mass democracy, their first priority that no decision be taken without everyone's knowledge and consent. Thus the meeting must be held at the height of summer, the only time when the enormous gathering, far too large to be accommodated in any existing Baba-i building, could take place in the open air without discomfort for the participants.

If these women, still fresh off the boat, still unfamiliar with and hostile toward this unyielding place, agreed about anything, it was that Lelaki had succumbed to mass megalomania. It was their most immediate concern that such a disease should not take root in their midst through the medium of the offspring. There were – food was still only just adequate – to be only some half-dozen children born a year; all were to be born at the same time to conserve resources. How were they to be brought up? Most were anxious that they not be left in the hands of the scientists responsible for their creation longer than was necessary to ensure their proper development as infants; this feeling arose from a prejudice that laid the ultimate blame for Lelaki technology at its originators' doors, with which originators the genetic engineers of Baba-i were felt to be allied in spirit. The meeting would not relinquish this stand, for all the arguments about the neutrality of a technology and the responsibility of its effects lying with its users; they had been deluded enough, they felt, by plausible scientific reasoning. Some other suitable way of bringing the offspring to maturity would therefore have to be found.

It might have seemed natural to allow the mother of each child to take her offspring away, off into whatever rough, benighted farmstead she or her companions had so far managed to inhabit on the bleak Baba-i moors. But many there, sitting in the watery sunshine, their topcoats folded under them against the reaching chill of a ground that never seemed truly to thaw, could remember all too clearly how, at home, men all around them had seemed to change, to become obsessed and doting about their offspring, ready to annihilate any obstacle even imagined to be in its path. Fear filled them, colder than the ground, at the thought of that happening here. There were those who believed, believed because they felt between themselves and the Lelaki an enormous and unbridgeable divide, that things must inevitably turn out differently in their case. Yet most could not muster such power of faith. There was enough about the conditions of life on Baba-i, their punishing but perhaps rewarding hardness, to remind them of the spirit nurtured amongst the first Lelaki settlers and invaders of old: that independent, conquering, pioneer spirit. Sending these children off into the wild, would they be raising, each in its pocket of isolation and trial, a national character that would one day blossom into the old Lelaki imperialism?

In the end those first offspring were raised by all (for everyone felt an obsessive need to check on their progress) and by none (for no one cared to get too close). The group of children travelled restlessly about the island, minded by whoever could be spared from the farmwork for the period of their stay, children into whose ears were poured a thousand prohibitions and exhortations, who absorbed the tithe of every adult's hatred for the Lelaki, who turned to each other for support and succour against the confusion of a hundred rearers, and against the suspicion that they met with from many who still saw them more as offspring than as Baba-i. The original settlers seemed to wish to distance themselves as much as possible from the first generations of offspring, to do everything in their power to enhance the differences between them. It was as if those rejected women of Lelaki had confidence neither in themselves nor in the new future that their stolen technology had brought; they would not seek to imprint themselves on their children, nor trusted themselves to envision another way of being toward which the offspring might be guided.

In later years the process of rearing became stabilized within the communities of the island, each settlement bringing up a batch at a time. The offspring grew up knowing intimately the contours of a particular landscape, as intimately as they knew each other. But the early distance, that sense of the new generation as dangerous and perhaps alien, seemed to linger, oddly replicated even by those who were themselves offspring.

Long after the first settlers had died, their cold bones hardly even memories around the homestead fires, the Baba-i offspring found themselves in possession of a culture whose concepts of evil were many, precise and well-articulated; they found that they knew clearly who not to be, but that positive images for the deliberate existence of Baba-i were lacking. There are those who claim that this fundamental absence lies at the heart of all Baba-i politics and philosophy, that their concern that they should not impose themselves, whether culturally or otherwise, upon other peoples is merely a result of a debilitating lack of self-confidence. This line of argument assumes, of course, that the Baba-i would be the Lelaki if they could, their refusal lying in incapacity rather than moral revulsion.

Another characteristic of the Baba-i that may be traced back to the conditions under which their ancestors suffered is their perpetual quest for knowledge or, failing that, information. At any one time perhaps one tenth of the active members of the community will be either abroad, gathering data, or engaged in the collation and analysis of material at home. Every news report, every scientific bulletin, each official and unofficial scrap is pored over in the libraries of Baba-i. While neither sheep nor fish farming is labour-intensive, and the pursuit of knowledge thus provides necessary employment, its primary use lies in quieting the national fear that without constant vigilance they will one day again be caught unawares by some shift in the order of the world. It is essential to the Baba-i character that they should be ready, not for their own moves, but for the moves of others.

Chapter 2

Eba: Entry #561

We were out with the sheep, most of us, when we heard the tractor grinding along the track, maybe a mile or two away. It was not that the sheep needed us, or that we needed the sheep; we were out because the sun was shining, after a week of rain, and because there was almost no wind. There is always wind, here. Calm is so rare that to wake in the morning to silence is to think yourself struck deaf in the night, or perhaps the earth stopped dead in its tracks. That it is not so everywhere, we – I – am of course aware. I have been out to other places. But you cannot remember silence, if you don't live with it. But we remember that day for the oddness of the weather.

There was plenty of time for everyone to have gathered in the outside courtyard, between the two barns, before the tractor arrived. We had guessed it was our batch, although we tend to come to meet anything that travels the road, naturally; however resourceful we may be we are not yet proof against novelty. I am among those who have suggested that it is this desire for the new that was our underlying motivation for bidding for the batch. The cynicism of this observation, while evident, in no way disallows its truth. I have always felt, moreover, that part of my responsibility as diarist, for the moment, of this muddy, rocky little farmstead, is to inject a little more scepticism into our inveterate self-examinations. Hope is always, it seems, making a bid for rebirth.

The sister driving the tractor could be seen waving as she came over the knoll and started down the track towards us.

"As if she's bringing gifts from afar," muttered Isul, her arms as usual wrapped around herself for warmth.

"Rather than a burden," I said.

"A trojan horse." There was a tight little knot of us now, elderly sisters sheltering under the lee of the haybarn, out of the wind from force of habit, and pronouncing our worst.

"There was something very odd about a culture that thought it rude to examine the teeth of a gift horse."

"Knew it was likely to bite, that's all," Isul said, and in that strange windless calm I could clearly hear the clacking of our ill-fitting dentures as we laughed.

There was a rush to examine the contents of the cart, even before the tractor had stopped. No one immediately touched anything, however: they leaned over the sides and looked at the well-wrapped bundles that someone had strapped to the sides of the cart with string. There was a pause, and the tractor engine stopped. None of the bundles moved; it seemed to me that they were waiting for some sign from us, some sign that it was quite likely that we knew nothing about. Or perhaps they were as dubious about us as some of us about them. The tractor driver said nothing, only sat in her seat watching us. They would be expecting a report from her, no doubt.

"Well, aren't we going to undo one, then? They must've got cold." There was a general movement to untie the string, although there was some argument about whether they would feel the cold more, or less.

"Think of lambs," the woman on the tractor said. Finally, Yani picked one up and set it on its feet in the cart. It staggered a little, very like a newborn lamb.

"How old is it?" Yani asked, looking at the woman on the tractor. The Librarians hold on to them longer all the time, or so rumour has it.

"Two," the bundle said. It sounded cross, and I felt more kindly disposed toward it on that account.

With that one word, there was a visible movement all round the cart, as if everyone had been rocked backwards by the force of it. I cannot say whether it was the otherness of these new creatures that so

81

shocked us, or whether on the contrary it was our first moment of recognition.

"Do you have names?" I asked. There have been complaints that I don't pay enough attention to names – indeed sisters are often adding to my diaries – the names of sheep, the names of which grasses are more abundant one year. I tell them it is the most futile of literary exercises, and they say that their interest is to record, whatever I may be doing. The bundles had all struggled out of their string and were standing up together in a bunch in the middle of the cart. The first one shook its head.

"We're sisters," another remarked significantly.

Isul cackled and poked me in the ribs, "How can they have names? They're fresh out of the machine."

We took them inside and put them in front of a fire (they were cold, it turned out). They seemed fascinated by the fire, and unfamiliar with its possibilities and dangers. They were no sooner set down on the floor than they began to waddle toward the flames in a body, making gurgling noises and throwing out their arms. Someone told them not to go too close to the fire but they seemed not to hear. It would not have occurred even to Isul in her rôle as messenger of doom that they might hear and choose to disobey, and so they were not so far from being roasted before a couple of younger sisters, perhaps with more flexible synapses, dragged them away.

"They did that deliberately," Jaimie said, standing between the three she had rescued and the green-flamed driftwood.

Our tractor driver put down the other, inanimate bundles that she had brought in the cart. "Sisters," she said, "didn't any of you go and do some research when you heard you were getting the batch?"

It did, in that moment, seem an odd omission. In discussing it later the sisters were anxious that I record their justifications. We did know a great deal about animal husbandry, and we knew a great deal more about ourselves; that, surely, gave us sufficient expertise to bring up the batch. As a sort of adjunct to this reason, no one had any particularly distinct memories of their own rearing being either complex or difficult. In our memory, a batch reared itself. Certainly, that is how we came to consciousness: we awoke to find ourselves looking at each other. It simply had not occurred to anyone that they had no information of the sort an adult might have acquired about their very earliest years; since our own batch are often the only children we ever see in twenty years, it is a state of things we tend not to theorize about. And then, we had simply wanted to believe that the batch could be managed without any great disruption of our routine, and without change. We needed younger sisters on the farm, able to take over more of the heavier work in a few years' time; and although we knew, how could we not, that integration of a batch is a matter of long effort and education, we had chosen to think that that problem could be pushed aside for the time being.

When our interpreting tractor driver had explained that the batch had not responded to a warning about the fire because they had not understood it in any immediate way, and we had established that this was not stupidity but normal human development, we arranged ourselves, as an interim safety measure, in a circle round them. It occurred to me, as we sat staring at them, that it is as well that Baba-i supports no predators large enough to make off with the spring lambs and we had hence no need to be out on the hillsides scanning for wolves. It is one of the few advantages to beggarly subsistence on a cold rock that, at almost all times of year, you may have leisure to sit and stare at something for as long as you choose.

"So it wasn't deliberate." Perhaps Mut felt faintly responsible for them, simply because she and Jaimie and Trac were next in age. Although any attempt at identification across a quarter of a century must be imperfect at best; she did not look as if she could remember a like inchoate state of mind. It is surprising how much one can forget and then forget even that one has forgotten. Perhaps to believe that we remember everything is the Baba-i version of spiritual pride. A necessary pride, if so.

"Could've been," said tractor sister, though it was coming to seem that she must be a batch-rearing expert, sent with them to make sure we weren't going to change our minds and drive them over a cliff. We would not have done that, of course – they were much too valuable. We would just have passed them along to wherever was next on the list for a batch, on condition that we could have first refusal on three when they grew up.

"Could've been," said tractor again, and she smiled. Next to me, Yani reached for my hand. Or perhaps I reached for hers. On the other side, Kit leaned into her shoulder. We waited.

"Kids!" tractor sung out suddenly. The batch, who had been lying in a heap together in the centre of our circle, looked at her.

"You don't always do as you're told, do you!" I was concentrating on her tone of voice. It reminded me of the croon you go into to calm a vengeful gull when collecting eggs. The batch giggled, and shook their heads and rolled about.

"They're anti-social," said Tim and Tam as one. Tom only nodded.

"Time and Tame have spoken," I said. It is an old joke, but their names irritate me. Siblings can be close enough without sounding like empty tunes. Isul laughed.

"Expose them on the hillside, then," screamed Alph, who had been sitting in the chimney corner all along, sorting seaweed. She lifted an arthritic hand and flung a shell that hit one of the batch on the head. They all started up a fitful, thin whining.

"You see? Nesh. Nesh lambs."

Our tractor driver was no longer smiling. I suppose that if you are not used to Alph it is she who would seem anti-social. Sometimes I wonder whether she is not merely fulfilling a rôle that we expect of her; she plays the crazed crone altogether too well.

"Oh, expose yourself," Jaimie said.

"Listen, all of you." We listened: it was a sufficiently impolite form of address to command our attention; and we felt that we had behaved badly.

84

"If — " the tractor's eye stared briefly at Alph, who continued tossing shells into the fire, "If you are a well-integrated group, for whom the idea of anti-social behaviour is almost unthinkable — " Isul raised her eyebrows at me during this rhetorical pause, "Then you should try to remember that this feeling is not natural. You were not born with it. You learnt it. If you do not teach it to these sisters, and if they do not see you carrying it out, then they will learn something else."

A shell exploded in the fireplace. Alph laughed as we all started: "Much better all die out, much better," she said.

Perhaps our sister of the tractor was reassured by the unanimity with which we all turned on Alph and told her to be quiet. At any rate she reached behind her and hefted one of the bundles into the circle, "The other bundles are spare cloth — they'll need new things quite often, especially at the beginning, when you'll find they grow fastest. This bundle is nappies. You'll have lanolin. This batch still use them, though it will probably only be for another few months."

I found Isul at the well.

"Bah," she said, "I thought at least they would come house-trained." We stood with our faces turned to the breeze. I think we found it reassuring, that soon the wind would be as usual. Isul and I rarely spend the hours of the long twilight outside. The cold is insidious, and the quality of the light seems to bring on sentimental indulgence; we will find ourselves thinking of Caro and shedding easy tears. It is always at these times that aging sisters are to be found in doorways, peering across the moor, muttering that they will go live with their siblings again, behind the eastern hills, or on the fishing station. We will never live anywhere other than where we are, of course. Even the lure of the lost batch-half, that foolish idyll of fulfillment, is not enough to drag our roots free; we are peasants, now, we are mired in peat up to our knees. We are a people of place, perhaps the more so because we were once so entirely displaced. We imagine that we still think and care about the world,

85

still worry and scheme over its doings as if they related to our own destiny. But as I look at us, old women fighting the sea and the hard grass for a bare living, I see us turning to earth ourselves.

Isul looked yellow in the twilight, and her cheekbones cast shadows. Soon it will be half the island's entire stock of morphine that the tractor will be bringing. She will have the little room that gets the morning sun, and everyone will insist that they depend on me to write our diary.

However. Inside, when I returned, the batch had been undressed and were asleep on a blanket. Somehow, their flesh came as a surprise; perhaps in an unexamined way I still thought of them as mechanisms while they were wearing layers of wool that might conceal wires. Of the six, five had hair in varying shades of brown and the dead white skin that this latitude requires for maximal absorption of sunlight. It is unusual, nonetheless, to see it over-represented so in a batch. No doubt someone did some fierce manipulation to get enough like that together so that someone else can wait and see whether they live longer. And if they do, of course, it will only be more knowledge acquired that we cannot use without moral anguish. They had been careful to vary the five of them as much as possible, otherwise. They had the look of systematically randomized faces. Because the eyes were closed I could only guess at their colour — but there will have been a decision that they should not all be blue. Or is that genetically impossible? Or against some other ethical rule? I no longer remember. Tirelessly we rebel against a uniformity from which there can be in reality no escape. The sixth had olive skin and that whiteblond hair. The sign here is unmistakable: it screams at us, it must be intended to scream at us. They send us five children perfectly adapted to life on the borders of the icecap, and one who looks like a Lelaki. To me, it is a sign without meaning.

Eba: Entry #733

The walls creak under the weight of this snow. If I look back to another winter I shall see that it is only the same, no heavier, no thicker, no longer-lasting. It is my patience that is running out, runs out faster every year. The old are not patient, they are only immobile, and enraged by it: Alph lies upstairs, spitting and snarling, furious all day and night. We have started keeping her in bed some of the time. That angry noise had begun to invade every corner of our minds.

Nearly everybody else is out in the barn, playing some ball game the rules of which I cannot be bothered to learn. I am told by the batch that this is a dereliction of duty, that the precise, arcane and intellectually delightful rules of this game should be recorded for the benefit of all – they have an obscene pride in their own invention. My recall of my own way of being at eight years old is sketchy, but it could have been then that we discovered how to do something with moss, cooking it so that a kind of perfume could finally be extracted. It was Caro who wrote it into the record. And I who recorded the fact that our distilled concoction went mouldy some weeks later, leaving a smell like decomposing rat flesh.

I wonder whether there have been genetic adjustments to provide a different temperament; I could go out there now and they might still be playing, hours after everyone else has retreated to sleep or read or quarrel over what to put in the stew, as if there were a choice. Or if they are not playing still, they will be sprawled in a heap over a hay bale, passing a turnip between them, as if this were what life were for, rustic bliss a shared turnip in a house turned into an igloo by the force of winter. They have patience, unnatural patience it seems to me – they do not seem to feel trapped. The rest of us do. Yesterday I found Lucia in with the sheep, screaming at them. After a while it became a joke, the argument she was having with them, and when they bleated she would respond as if they had offered a suggestion or a protest, albeit a stupid one, and she started laughing at them. But that is not how it began: she went in there murderous, and murderous because in the kitchen someone had suggested that that was a wasteful way to be doing with the dried parsley, that after all would have to last a while yet. We are all precarious, standing on the brink of something that might be disintegration, if there were any way left of judging.

And Isul is dying, damn her. I go in every morning and we upset one another; it is a routine we have developed. "Here's the vulture," she remarks to Jaimie or whoever, conversationally, "tell her I'm still alive." Then she likes to flap her arms and squeak, "No pickings! No pickings yet!" It could be the morphine, but it is also the logical extension of Isul's habit of mistrust, her doubt that we all shared and fed off, grown monstrous. Her body is thin, shrunken, she has lost control of its functions; she is dying gracelessly and slowly. It is as we had predicted, except that she had in mind to die well on in spring when movement is possible again. As it is I shall not even be able to get outside to burn her for another two months. She will have to wait in the snow until then. If I still recognized Isul, I might wonder if the idea of standing frozen sentinel over the house might not rather appeal to her; she will finally become an object of terror, even if only to the batch. I crossed over to the northeastern fell once, just on thaw, to a house where there were three frozen corpses stacked outside waiting for firing. They could have been logs of wood, the especially thick ones used at the back of the fireplace sometimes, except for glimpses of leathery faces through the ice. I promised myself that I would die in summer, then, when the air is clear and the bones are dry and the smoke will be thin and light. I was still there when they burned those women. They burned them all together, still wet with winter cold, and the hillside around smelt of slow roasting and the gallons of sheep fat they had used to get the pyre going for a week afterwards.

* * *

Batch Observation: Arrival

The batch have been physically examined. Their fourteenth birthday will fall in the next summer quadrant, and their development is generally appropriate to this stage in the growth cycle. No abnormalities are apparent.

This is the first batch to be reared by the Eastern Fell Farm. The isolation of this particular settlement is reflected in certain physical traits acquired by the batch. They all have above average physical strength ratings, and show high stamina capacities for their age group. On the other hand, they have not attained the height predicted in the Batch Programme, and menarche occurred only one month ago, instead of in the first winter quadrant of their thirteenth year, as expected. The Eastern farm is the only one that has no fishing station of its own, or relatively easy access to one during times of unsnow. The initial hypothesis is that the indwellers suffer from a mild dietary deficiency that results from the absence of fish. Further investigation will be necessary, however. It is not immediately clear why the seaweed that is a routine element in their diet should not be an adequate substitute. The Eastern Fell is not landlocked, naturally, but no fish farm has been established there due to the turbulence of the waters off the Eastern shore. (Refer: fish farm experimental records.) It is also possible that a sheep-based life cycle results in either a different developmental cycle or an altered outcome; batch growth rate predictions have inevitably been based on previous experiments, all of which featured some degree of childhood exposure to fish farming. Does the element of time spent out at sea on the spawning platforms affect growth rates or types in some way?

Some of the same questions may arise in analyzing the batch psychological data, although here there are more variables in play. The batch are, on initial observation, within parameters for adjustment. They are, in the immediate stages of arrival and acclimatization at the Library, both wary and curious. Again, it should be borne in mind as observations progress that the Eastern Fell is marginally less hospitable even than other regions of Baba-i: these offspring have spent their lives in an environment where one's first concern must always be with self-protection of the most immediate kind, of fragile ill-adapted flesh against the cold.

They are, unsurprisingly, fascinated and slightly

repelled by the technological devices, crude as they are, that enable Librarians to dispense with the dailiness and the anxieties of warmth and life maintenance. Their curiosity, however, is more wide-ranging; first assessments suggest that they feel a relief at the possibility that the Library offers of there being more to life, even for us, than the struggle to harvest enough turnips and stave off frostbite.

It is too early to say whether hostility will be a problem. The variables here would seem to be the specifics of the environment, and the particular genetic manipulations instituted prebirth. These remain, of course, startling upon initial encounter; and it would also seem as if the batch continue to be aware of their unrandomized pigmentation, that it continues to present a psychological difficulty for them. Given the superficial nature of this manipulation, however, it seems unlikely that their appearance can have had or can continue to have any lasting internal effect. It is possible, however, that it may have influenced, in ways perhaps not programmed for, the attitude of the farm indwellers to the batch.

Internal Memo: Arrival

They were cold, as always after journeys. They went first to the air vent; despite the novelty of this means of heating, they warmed themselves carefully, making sure that the temperature of the extremities did not change too quickly. They then discussed the likely means of production of such quantities of hot air, but without arriving at the possibility of water power. They did not ask for clarification on this point, although a Librarian was present and available, nor did they consult either a reference index or a terminal, both of which are of course immediately accessible in the common room. (A sift indicates that these failures – to pursue avenues of enquiry – are standard features in batches returned inlibrary after rearing.) Routinely, the habit of enquiry is encouraged by rearers but the means to problem-solving is conceptualized in the fells in terms of practical experimentation. Thus, of the hot air emerging from a vent, a batch was heard to remark,

90

upon removing the vent cover, "I can't see where it's coming from." As if a visual clue, and only a visual clue, would have enabled her to solve the mystery. (It might surely be worth considering how much intellectual potential is at least delayed and perhaps even aborted due to the long period during which batches are not subject to proper mental training. We ought not to waste brains who do not waste anything else.)

They did then turn to the shelves and begin to explore their possibilities. Their exploration was without pattern, or rather had the pattern of random sampling. They were not processing information, but reading out to each other snips and bites from any sources they happened upon. Possibly they felt secure in the assumption that the resource now available to them would not immediately be removed and that they were free to play. They became, within an hour, hysterical with it. (A sift and personal anecdote both suggest that this too is normal.)

Internal Memo: Arrival

Some batch comes in from the cold every spring, about this time. We could mark the season shift by it, but we don't. I was wondering why we don't, it's as regular as the other cycles even Librarians live by. We were walking down to the store sheds, only yesterday, and Ruth stopped dead, I thought an idea had come on her. Then she raised her head and swivelled her neck and wrinkled up her nose, "The mackerel are moving." A half arrested on the path, snuffing the wind like seals. And we knew it was spring so.

Of course it's rare that a half should have to bring in the batch more than once, so it never comes to have seasonal meaning for us personally. But we all know when it happens, we all avoid the common rooms so they don't get too much casual contact, we all watch them from a distance and feel glad and sorry for them – the batch's been brought, spring must be here? No?

We dread it, how not? The awful wholeness of that group, its total cheerful self-satisfaction, it drives you crazy with longing and disgust.

* * *

Tab: Entry#1

The cart jerked about too much to write while we were travelling. And the others were noodling under the blanket, and distracting me. And then the pen stuck to my fingers, so I gave up. Not that it was so good under the blanket – we went into a pothole and Ebony rolled over and almost crushed my hand.

I got landed with this. I didn't choose it. I didn't even give in gracefully. We drew sticks three times and I lost every time, but I still know I shouldn't be doing it. You're supposed to want to chronicle, after all. We don't know anything at all, so it's a mystery to me how we can have anything worth saying – all right, sisters?

I give you a list: I am homesick. Ebony is homesick. Tea is homesick. So are Gertrude, Alice and White. We don't know quite what it is we're missing, though. Can't be mother, can it. We rather think the farm will be glad to see us gone. Until, Tea says, the water runs out and they start having to go to the well again. And the firewood, too. What will they do without their hewers of wood and drawers of water? Everyone, Alice says, will put their backs out and retire to bed, Or pretend to put their backs out. Meanwhile, we are going to chop no wood, and we're not going to the well for anyone else, and we're going to read everything in the Library. Then we're going to see the world.

Tab: Entry#13

The wind generators here are big enough to pump the water and make hot air for heating. Alice has been making technical drawings for months and is only reading engineering textbooks. She thinks she is going to save the farm from itself by freeing it from drudgery. Or that is what she pretends to think. Maybe she's worried that if we don't come up with something practical soon we'll be sent home to the vegetable patch to cultivate lichen.

We watch ourselves all the time for signs of

integration. It having dawned that they don't let a batch loose on the Library and let them play without some purpose in mind, since this isn't Lelaki and we have nothing to spare . . . Alice, of course, seems well won over to socialization. I have been reading the records, our records. Hence the terminology. There's a great deal of fascinating stuff, most of it quite frightening when you realize that when they arrived our ancestors had no idea at all what they were doing. Anyone, you might say, can get over uncertain beginnings. Ordinary people can't've had much notion of what they were for, for a few million years. They seem to have just existed, and made up the reasons why they were doing it a particular way as they went along. All the texts say that they were convinced, at the time. And now there they are, out there, still getting on with it, and trying to pretend that the randomness of their stories doesn't matter, or else that it's really all the same story underneath. Only the Baba-i with the problem.

Tea said, was there any record of a sister ever getting God? I can't find anything, though it could be done, I reckon. It would have to be the whole batch, of course, They would just decide one day that they'd been put here for a purpose, and off they'd go. It's what they'd decide their mission was that I can't see. Tea's opinion is that the only sensible one would be world domination. First you create a super race and then you conquer everyone else, quickly, before they can do the same to you. Tea seems to think this stands or falls according to whether there's enough spare capacity at the laboratory to produce an army that fast. It's interesting to watch the Librarians, when Tea gets off on this. Well, Tea starts and then we all pick it up and orchestrate – you know how easy that is – and the Librarians are looking at one another and meanings are charging about all over the place, and then they all start in, though not all the same, because they're two half-batches and they don't have our sync; but the point is, how seriously they take us. As if it's finally arrived, the batch that's going to threaten Life As We Know It.

Tab/Stone: Entry#51

Suddenly name changes seem important to everyone. It's obvious from the records that things were simpler when you were given something at birth and stuck with it. Everyone just adapted themselves to their name and stability was ensured . . . not that I'm not glad that Gertrude has been stripped off, although Esmé is only more of the same. Esmé/Gertrude maintains that this one keeps the intellectual quality and disposes of the rustic. I wait to see what the farm will say. In fact I know what they'll say, they'll say it sounds like a sheep in difficulties. Ebony has in fact done the same thing. We seem to be looking for the absurd. She would have had Teak, if Tea hadn't ruined that, and has ended, or settled for now, maybe, on Redwood. These siblings are embarrassing. Now White feels compromised, of course, and I'm thinking of renaming myself Blush Pink and Tea says she could go for Warrior Purple. In truth I'm disgusted to see us so transparently going through a stage of developmental trial and error. It ought to be fascinating to watch us, I realize, fieldwork before your eyes, but I'd rather we just missed out on a little of this predictable experimentation.

White is still obsessed with the Lelaki; she at any rate doesn't progress, she just goes further in. What her research actually reveals is that, the more you know, the less like a real Lelaki she seems. She looks like that, of course, or rather, to be precise, she has the hair, the eyes and the skin tone. Her body is all wrong: it's short and rather solid and slightly longer in the body than the leg. One of them would know the difference at a hundred yards. And so ought we, is the point. White's theory is that this way of judging people is part of our ineradicable (Lelaki, naturally) heritage, so that she exists to serve us right and act as an awful warning. Very early on, almost the first thing we did, was go to the laboratory and look out our programmes. Even for us, then, it was easy to see that we weren't randomly selected. Well, there were always those at the farm who said you could tell that, just by looking. I used to like to think they'd

94

controlled some things and let the dial spin on others, since dial-spinning is one of those early moral tenets that get handed down in touching memorial fashion. But there's no trace of it in the Batch Directions. Well, of course that's not true – all they've done, you might say, is decide the way we look. They don't have the knowledge to control a lot else, apart from a few nasty diseases. Or they say they don't. But the question really is, isn't it, what controlling the way we look finally ends up controlling. Is it just White it has the big effect on? So she's the one that you'd find an old sister staring at, some winter noon, and the one that named herself years early, to stop sisters from calling her something else, or not knowing what to call her. But then, as a batch, not only do we have her, we have the rest of us, at once too different and too alike. The half-batches on the farm, they just look different, but within some sort of given range. We are not like that. We have been looking at ourselves, and looking at others looking, and looking at ourselves looking, ever since our eyes opened. I – or the half-batch of us that were there – said to the Librarian, why make us a walking text book. A way of inscribing what we are doing, of getting us to look at what it is, she said. That's what I thought, I said, you can call me Tablet of Stone from now on, to be abbreviated to Stone. I like our new half: Stone White Tea has a menacing sound.

Stone: Entry#59

Esmé complains that I write from my point of view. Try writing it from somewhere else, I said. There you are again, she said, making out our half is hopelessly naive. She wants things set down, everything set out, as if records could be like that, if you only did them well enough. She wants me to be able to write as her, as if we were all still three years old and could laugh at each other's jokes without their having to be said out loud. Esmé is in revolt against personality, she thinks it's something we could probably get rid of, if we tried. She claims that the Library really just exists in order to manufacture difference. We were having this argument, all of us, walking backwards and forwards in the shed by the airstrip, because Red thought the supply plane might still land, unless the snow got worse. And so there we were, criss-crossing over the floor, couldn't stop moving for the cold, making a neat pattern that you would've been able to see best from the ceiling. We can still do this, Red had said, pointing it out, and so we had gone on walking and Esmé was introducing spontaneous variations to see whether we all followed, and we were all laughing, as if we were still little after all, and being each other were enough. This is what you want, is it, Tea said, that we follow one another like sheep? Alice and Esmé defend the integrity of sheep against Tea and White who say, of course, all they do is baa, how should they disagree, and I am saying, how do you know they agree, what's all that conversation about if it's not bickering; and we suddenly come to a dead halt in the middle of this cold draughty shed, the rhythm of the dance quite gone.

Nobody tells us anything, probably that's the only cardinal principle of bringing up a batch that is still operative. I look at the Librarians, sometimes, sitting there blandly, expectantly, so ready to have an enlightening conversation, always quick with the repartee but never initiating anything. Does the urge to warn us about something in advance never come over them? Do they never think, poor batch, we'll just give them a little preparation for the next shock? I know what they'll say, we don't believe in Guides and Leaders of Youth, do you? Really though, would it have been imposing foreknowledge, if we had not grown up assuming that that unthinking harmony would last for ever?

So there we are in the shed. Big moment. Looks like we all have to admit we're not sheep, White says. Abandon the safety of the uncontentious animal world. Baa no more. Only sheep agree, is that it, Esmé screams. Looks like it, Tea remarks, and there we are. The sheep faction on one side of the room, and the three of us on the other. We still have our halves, I said. No doubt there's a rustic saying for this occasion, Alice said. We abandoned the plane and went home trying to make one up. Better a half-batch than an ice floe in winter. If you carry six eggs in your pocket, three will break.

Stone: Entry#65

They are going back, the sheep half, that is. We don't know when, yet. Perhaps the Librarians do; perhaps it always takes a batch exactly so many months to leave each other. I could look it up, of course, of course, but I don't want to. Instead the three of them spend a lot of time standing in the half-light, looking at the snow, and we stand next to them, just for the sake of it. Or we will be in the Library, at a table, and we look up and we are all staring at one another with a sort of blank intensity. Then someone will ask one of those questions. Doesn't the farm call you, Red asked me. The cry of the sheep across the moor, I would've said, being Tea. Doesn't the rest of the world call you, I would've said, being White. What kind of question is that, I said, being me. I'm trying to give you information, Red said, for your records. The Librarians seem worried, that the sheep half is not recording itself. It seems to want not to exist, letting me write as if I could still feel the whole batch. We want to be the farm, is what Alice said, as if this were overwhelmingly evident and explained everything.

Stone: Entry#73

Alice drove the tractor, although it should've been a Librarian for symmetry, the Return of the Batch. You forget how uncomfortable that cart is, how you bang your head against the sides when it lurches. It rained, of course, icy spring rain, and it's too early yet for the snow to be off the track. Too early to be travelling in a cart.

But there they all were, standing outside, staring up the hill towards us. Just dark bundles against the snow, staring as if the Lelaki might be coming down on the fold. I was glad I wasn't coming home, but the sheep half didn't seem to notice, it seemed to be what they were expecting. But I have given up pretending to know what the sheep are thinking.

They put us in front of the fire and we all gazed at it. Obviously, it was burning driftwood that we were homesick for all along. Eba was in the chimney corner, watching us watch the flames. Always liked the fire, she said, didn't you, batch. She looked no older than I remember, except she has stopped wearing her teeth. She looked at us in that way that means she still writes the records. If there is anything to say about this farm, aside from the birth of animals and the death of old women. But she looked, and I asked, anything to record, sister?

Eba: Entry#856

I'm past this, as she well knows. The return of the half-batch; I find little enough to say about it. I can find it in me to be glad that there will be young women here: the roof needs mending, and shovelling snow is strenuous work. The years have only increased my feeling of distance from the batch. At least as babies they did not have expectations; now they look at me as if there is something they want. They have been practising tolerance while they have been away. They do not turn away when I drool, or when I spit in the fire and my aim is faulty. The one who records, she almost cannot look for all that she has the habit, in her eagerness to be away. That half has decided to believe that the truth lies elsewhere. I am a little surprised to find that I cannot even summon a little brittle warmth of fellow feeling for their desire to see the world. But I cannot seem to find it in me to despise the ones who have come cheerfully back, determined to be peasants, either. As individuals we are incomplete conduits for emotion, it would appear. It is fortunate for our mental health, no doubt, that this lack is only fully apparent when the siblings are dead. If I had had to spend my middle-age having imaginary conversations with Isul and Caro before I could work out what I was thinking, I should have been tempted by the Crag long since. When I might have been able to contemplate walking there. As it is, it is only now I realize that I needed Isul to articulate that rejection of the rural calm that is how I – not Isul, or Caro – feel.

Or felt, since I no longer in fact can. We felt something of this, naturally, when Caro died, a loss of a range of feeling. But somehow we held off the loss: she was there, still, in our knowledge of her, because it was shared. Finally I understand – it is much too late – why we go back, at the end, to hankering for the half-batch that we lost fifty years ago, why Alph would hobble off towards the southern fishing station, and why before her Sophie would try to climb the hill behind the house in search of phantoms. It is because we are husks, without our siblings, but husks that remember what the liquid of understanding felt like, giving us body, flesh beneath the carapace.

This batch, then, sitting in front of what I now tend to think of as my fire, sitting all day chewing seaweed and nuts as if determined to display for me all the things I can no longer eat: it is hard to believe that they have declared themselves competent, of age; their notions are as untried and dangerous as the day that they first arrived and almost roasted themselves alive in the fire. Or perhaps I am only too accustomed to being able to predict, exactly, what any sister will have to say on whatever subject. The batch have come from the Library stuffed with speculation, even the ones who are to stay. They spend their hours redesigning the house and our lives in one seamless, fantastical band. Meanwhile, the ones who are to go are a little reluctant to leave, and the ones who are to stay cannot bear to lose their link with the world. They spent the afternoon in a bed designed to hold no more than three, directly above my head. I could hear all their little noises, even before they began to laugh hysterically and baa like a flock of sheep.

Stone: Entry#83

We were standing on the dock, watching seals out in the bay. And this is what passes for summer, Tea said. As if we already knew what summer was really like. Think enough about it and you're over there already. Drinking cold drinks, and looking for shade. White says she is going to wear a bikini and a straw hat. Even if we end up going to someone else's winter, she says. We spend hours watching films, of anywhere that is not here. The Librarians hand out the cassettes and make notes, overlooking our lack of organization. They can only be waiting for us to recover from losing the sheep half, they have that knowing glance to them that says we are going through another necessary procedure.

So, we were standing on the dock, and Tea was complaining about the weather, and White said she thought we should go soon, the technology was bound to break out somewhere. How could we know what to do, unless we knew where it was? It's a tribute to the Librarians' skill that I hadn't realized how far we'd come until it was much too late. There we were, suddenly, fully integrated members of the community. Talking about what the Baba-i always talk about, as if it was something to do with us, and as if we were going to do something about it. What's the matter, Tea said, you've gone a bit green. I explained that I had just realized that we were socialized and that there was no escape from anything. White looked pleased, as if she had been hoping it would happen soon, so that we would be let out to do our bit. Well, Tea said, it's inevitable. Doesn't mean we aren't going to change the way things are done. White said, didn't I know it was a con all along. They probably write acquiescence into our genetic code. Or should I say, we.

The Librarians looked smug. And then occasionally they would smile enormously, as if they had been keeping back a laugh for five years. What's with you, Tea said to them, you must've known we'd come round. Then the Librarians looked at each other — more than once, as if they couldn't quite make up their mind — and said, there was always the possibility. Choosing to be an outsider among the Baba-i, White said, no one needs to go out that far. And where would you go else, I said. Well, said the Librarians, here you are. I'd say it was the silliest, most self-congratulatory conversation I've heard since we got into the home brew at the farm when we were six. It was just the same. That day we thought we had the world in our hands.

Chapter 2

Maria: Entry#477

I am in receipt of your 'advice', as you call it. There is really no need for you to reiterate the theoretical basis underlying the decision to send us into the field alone. I am quite well aware of the theory. The problem is that it doesn't work.

I don't know how you can expect it to. Do you keep data, back there, on whether it ever really works? Well, you must. It wouldn't be like you to pass up an opportunity for information gathering – but you might have a problem about who to send. It would be throwing good sisters after bad, wouldn't it. I know you're very sophisticated about the interaction between the observer and the observation, you would expect contamination. The third truth, one of you used to say, that which is created in the meeting of the viewer and the viewed. Beautiful, it used to sound.

Perhaps it does sometimes work. Maybe I'm just an aberration. It used to sound plausible enough even to me. You used some sheep analogy or other, didn't you, about how the orphan lamb makes an adaptation to another mother, makes it because it has to. How somewhere in the blurry infant sheep brain the synapses shift and quiver and new pathways open up, and lambkin sees itself and the world from another relation, another identity. You would get quite high flown about it, for you. Quite overtaken with the missionary zeal about how we would go out into the unknown of other cultures and imitate lambs. How the naked individual, stripped of her batch, would take on the way of seeing of those she walked among, unconscious act of necessity and self-conscious strategy for comprehension all at the same time. I may have got

101

pretty odd, over here, but I haven't forgotten what it is you believe happens.

Except that from here it feels more like lamb to the slaughter. Doesn't that make you a little uncomfortable, sisters? Aren't we supposed to be against sacrifice, to be a bit sceptical of cleansing violence, given our history?

Taking me out would not be the point. For one thing, it doesn't solve the problem that your whole theory is screwed up. For another, when I say that I'm going crazy, out here by myself, it isn't that I can't see anything. It's just that I can't merge with them and I can't be anyone I recognize . . . you don't have to send me my batch-half – that would be indulgent, wouldn't it – but you could send someone. It would be more efficient.

I can hear you being unconvinced. Yesterday I was at a meeting, I'll try and describe it. There are four women there and me. This is a middle-class crowd, we're in the city, and they're social workers, journalists, a teacher. They iron their clothes and their hair is glossy. They are the privileged here – at home they take for granted gadgets that we hardly think about. Hair dryers, just the small stuff. And they probably grew up with maids, or at least someone who came in to clean the house. So make an effort, you say, make a leap. And I do – my clothes are almost chic, I tell you. It's not camouflage that's hard.

This is a strategy meeting, they're here to discuss what policy should be adopted about the sugar conference. No one's going to let them in, naturally, only the old barons and the Lelaki are going to be round that table, licking each other's boots and dividing up the profits. But they need to know what the demonstrators outside should be saying, because that will get reported too, and they have to say the right thing to the people. The line from their friends in the hills is about land reform, and the barons and the colonialist intruders are much the same evil as far as they're concerned, an evil that needs expelling. That's the revolutionary position, says Natalia, it must be heard. Then she smooths her skirt and says, yet we must not alienate the professional classes. Tobi nods, we must respect legitimate aspirations. And they all murmur respectfully. Cherrie is the journalist, and she explains this to me. Revolution does not mean stepping back into the darkness, the time before progress and industrialization. The peasants look to the progressive middle class for rôle models, for hope. The colonists have brought many advantages – why give up the few benefits they have provided, what little return there has been for their exploitation of the Islands. Tobi manicures her hands, I suppose somebody else, in fact, manicures her hands. They flutter, as if it is the fan stirring them. Her pupils, she tells me, are full of the romance of the outside world. Of course this has to be questioned, they must be brought to see that glamour is a cover for exploitation – but all the same. She laughs, and her polished nails flicker; not all progress can be dismissed as decadence. The modern world is ours too, she says. Natalia spends her days in the shantytowns, she has taken me along with her there, and I would expect her to say that, mostly, the modern world that the Islanders have known is squalor and disease, the underside of urban sophistication where so many more people actually live. And she is frowning, as if she is about to lay bare Tobi's complicity. She shrugs. I wish it were ours, she says, this world.

And where is our lamb in all this? Juanita doesn't trust me so she is the one who watches me. She has been watching me during this conversation, and now she says, you will never understand, because you do not understand desire. Of course, this is partly a wilful misunderstanding on her part, a refusal to accept my readiness to be protean, to understand anything. But partly she is right: I am supposed to understand *that*? Did you think you were bringing up beings of infinite flexibility, is that really our Librarians' goal? But that isn't the point. The point is that analogy will take us only so far. I may be lamblike in some respects – hard not to be, growing up with hardly anyone else to talk to – but I'm not one. This is presumably a good idea. I rarely meet a Baba-i sheep on a fact finding mission in the Islands. Sisters, the point is that I can be them, sometimes, I can look along the lines of vision of these Island women, sometimes – but I can't want what they want. Can't. Not unless mutton can think itself pork, but even that is wrong. I can think myself pork, but I can't think myself porcine desires. Juanita thinks I want nothing, or nothing that is worth wanting, in which she is entirely wrong. I only don't want the Lelaki. Send me a sister, please, because I feel flayed.

Meanwhile, they are everywhere. It seems to me, although I have only anecdotal evidence of this, that their numbers are increasing. Or it could just be a few of them getting about a whole lot more. Probably not – they seem so very leisured. They sit about, they lounge in every cafe, as if the Islands were some enormous R & R playground. And they smile. They smile, and they flick locks of blond hair back from their dark fine-chiselled faces. They are very beautiful. Even I can see this – or, I can see this by being a lamb. I watch the women here watch them. It's not that they don't hate them. In a way that's easy, they can afford to hate them and even to let it show, sometimes. Even the women in the bars will risk a sneer. But then I see the way the corners of their eyes crinkle when one of them goes past, his body so lithe and long and yet understated. It's not the sexual attraction that I mean. They don't want him, they want what he has – they want the thin miasma that comes out of his pores, that surrounds him. It can't be that they want just to be that way – no one here has any difficulty seeing the Lelaki as dangerous and devious and too powerful to trust, and you don't copy something you need to circumvent. I suppose I'm frightened of them because they're plausible, and there's something attractive about what plausibility can do for you.

Maria: Entry#478

I get very tired of your little ways. Your little attempts to achieve godlike flicks of poetic justice. Please refrain, in future, from treating me as an experiment or as if I were some naive of fairytale. So you send me a sister, but a sister who looks like one of

104

them. My, how witty. My, how chastening. Did you ask her how she felt about being the living embodiment of some abstruse point?

I am taking her about to see the sights, as this seems to be what she expects. But this is not the time for tourist diversions. I am going to leave the city, there are places where I think other things are going on. Places where the blond boys are not yet maggot thick on the ground.

You should send my supplies to Sister Maria from now on. That isn't camouflage, of course. Just my own little joke.

* * *

White: Entry#1

We arrive in a downpour, a raining not like home at all, sudden and thick and still too warm. All this water has nowhere to go and lies on the road in a great sheet, a lake, which our taxi goes through all the same, part of a huge swerving mass of buses and cars hurtling into the city half under water. I cling close to this unfamiliar sister who has collected me and she to me, I think, though she is pretending to be cosmopolitan and explaining that, simply, this is another Lelaki colony bound into the values and economics and forms of pollution that the Lelaki themselves have long since abandoned for sanity and environmental regulation. When the rain stops I realize that it has been keeping the overpowering diesel fumes at bay and that the normal air you breathe here is thick and lies chokingly on your lungs and your brain.

She takes me to somewhere where, she says, tourists do not go. From the roadway the buildings lean out towards us like the mazy house of cards a bored child builds on the farmhouse floor on a slow afternoon, all overlapping layers of thin wood and corrie, and random walls. She holds my hand over the stepping stones and twists and turns along mud alleys as if she knows where we are going. In one of these dark places we are given a hot beige liquid, powerfully sweet, that sister says is evaporated milk and coffee, and is drunk so that you can feel life in your veins. I feel the rush of sugar singing in my head. As we drink and sister explains me in some mixture of languages that I seem only half to remember, around us people sleep at odd angles across the floor. It reminds me of an autumn gathering at home when the company all hives into the one room for warmth and gradually there are bodies curling up to sleep in all the chairs and corners. Only here perhaps they have the necessity, with so many of them, everywhere.

She finds us somewhere to stay, in a room one floor above the wet dark of the alleys. She sits across from me and says, she doesn't know what we are doing here. We must only roam about over the Islands and see, but she does not expect we will know what we are looking at. That does not matter, I say, because at home they will be able to understand, that is why I have been sent, to describe it all for them. I am not expected to interpret. She tells me that I know nothing, that I do not even realize that I do not know, and that therefore I am useless. While we talk a constancy of different sounds breaks in through the wooden slats of the window, crying and laughter and something that might be gunshot in the distance and the banging of cooking pots. Sister says, she had thought I had been sent to companion her, and not she me, and she is nobody's bodyguard. She lies the rest of the evening in silence and will not tell me where we are going. She has acclimatized and will not bear the noise of the fan, and so I must lie and sweat and think of our cold with longing.

White: Entry#2

Sister takes me downstairs and shows me where to wash. The toilet is like the ones the Lelaki supplied us at the beginning, that require sitting on. But this is only how it looks, for there is no water in it. That must be collected from a tap under the sink and poured

106

onto your shit. Sometimes, sister tells me, this results in it going successfully into the drains. I would rather do things some other way, but she explains that there is no choice and we are fortunate to have any water at all. While I am away down there sister has dressed, and I notice that there is some slight change about her dress that I cannot quite pin down. She tells me that it is a necessary disguise. The less odd we look the better. But she does not tell me who it is we are pretending to be. My clothes are of Baba-i and I can see, looking at sister, that I am not going to pass. Already she is pretending that I am going to be a real trial to her and that she would be better off by herself.

White: Entry#5

All day she takes me about from office to office, explaining that we have come on behalf of our government to see things for ourselves, the things their government will not show us. Sister produces letters of recommendation from other offices in other countries and the people in these offices nod and ask us what we would like to see, as if they have everything at their command, could lay the country out before us, a tapestry of truth. Sister lowers her voice and looks into their eyes with meaning and says she would like to see how things are going out there. Their eyes slide in turn across the table at me as if they somehow do not know quite who I am, and they whisper that a certain level of exposure can be arranged.

We travel on little diesel buses, inching the streets in a pall of grey fumes. Breathing is a necessary act of suicide. Around me everyone is smoking cigarettes, as if choice of a personal poison inures them to the one that seeps into them from every particle of air. On the journey sister names the city to me, underpasses, overpasses, some fetid river where more card-house dwellings hang over sick grey water. She threatens to leave me somewhere to find my own way back to our room, a flood of directions and street names reeling out of her mouth; she is waiting for me to say that she is unsisterly, unbearable, but I do not rise to her bait, knowing she is only having trouble with how essential we are, each to the other. There are times when the carefully nurtured Baba-i interdependence is an incubus riding evil on your shoulder. I stop in the street and shake myself, as if to loose its grip.

In the evening sister seeks out old friends, or contacts – the distinction is hard for me to draw – and we meet them in an old high-ceilinged house, a great hall downstairs with polished wood floors and a sense of space that already feels foreign and luxurious. Afterwards sister explains to me the existence here of a more or less prosperous class whose allegiance either side must still fight for. The people that we meet here are all part somehow of organizing women, as I understand it, although neither sister nor anyone else is able to say this to me directly. Little is said about anything, directly: the air is full of anecdotes that have some meaning, and speaking looks. I gather I am being told more than I understand, or than I have any right to expect. Mostly I sit in silence and watch. It is the first time since leaving home that I have sat in a room filled only with women, and automatically I find myself more comfortable, relaxed, as if these too are my sisters. I seem to feel this kinship despite their own unease with me; when I am introduced one of them puts her head on one side and asks lightly, Lelaki? Sister laughs and says, that is sometimes how we look, and they are graceful and smile, and accept me because I am sister's. As they talk I look between them and sister and I see how it is that sister is disguised: she has become one of them, in the half-light of the lamp even her skin colour will not pick her out from among them. She bends, gestures, laughs as they do. I cannot say what she has done to her clothes, except that perhaps they are brighter and they seem to show her body beneath them in a way we do not. But the difference is less than I expected; these women, telling stories of the struggle, do not seem to have the marks on them of a sex burdened and distorted by dimorphism, they seem complete. Except perhaps that they will not take me as I am. They cannot see beneath the colour of my hair and so they look away.

108

White: Entry#8

Sister spends hours, days, meeting people of whom I can recall only that they represent some faction or other, some interest group. There seem to be a dozen divisions, by economic group or occupation and then again into two sections by sex. Or rather there is a main organization, and alongside that a women's section. Sister behaves as if this were quite ordinary. It is bizarre, this manifestation of different interests between men and women that still presumes that they have ends in common. I am rebuked for suggesting that there is false consciousness in their common cause; sister accuses me of imperialism and of having the dust of the Library in my brain. It is true that it is harder than I thought, not to want to intervene, to tell them what you know, what you see. Sister claims, swilling her hot beige coffee around her glass, that we have much more in common with the Lelaki than we – and me in particular, naturally – like to think. She continues to treat me as a troublesome innocent, a thing younger not only than her years but also immature for my own, although I have reminded her that my innocence is professional, a describer's openness to impressions. Sister appears wilfully to confuse this receptiveness with a blank sheet on which the world, and she, may write as they wish. Her attitude is patronizing, and I am working myself up to an accusation of deliberate obstructiveness, despite my intentions to bear with these tendencies of hers. She has been away from home too long, too long alone. If I am too innocent, she would appear to have been thoroughly corrupted. Her name, for now, she tells me, is Maria.

White: Entry#13

I am lying on the wooden floor, the fan at my feet. The rain is still beating on the wooden slats, turned flat to keep out the water and thus barely filtering the light. Sister says we are waiting for the wind, that it may yet slap down on the city from the eastern sea, tearing our neighbours' houses leaf from leaf. Perhaps it is the fan's turning of the air or the sound of determined rain that makes me shiver in the heat. Or the afternoon. We have been out on the streets, hurrying as usual from place to place. Someone tells sister that rain is forecast and a typhoon coming, and she takes no notice except to say, as we get on and off buses, that we ought to have brought an umbrella. But she is abstracted, all anticipation, until we come to a road junction that seems to me no different. We both stand there, Maria looking at me sidelong and saying she wished I had bothered to be less conspicuous; still she has not told me how to blend in with this crowd. I look at the junction and suddenly the traffic has been stopped and the road is blocked by police trucks. Crowd barriers are being taken out of the backs of vans. Sister nudges me and points back the other way, far down the road. Behind the buses and the diesel haze that still streams towards us, there is a brighter blur. A women's demonstration, sister says, and she drags me away from the kerb into a shop doorway in case we should seem too interested.

The rain has started as they come down towards us, a small crowd of them, running along the road as if they fear being caught from behind, or surrounded. They are waving orange and pink flags, their shouting sounding ragged as the rain catches them, beating them into the tarmac. As they reach the junction and the road block they stop running and stand tight together. The chanting pitches out louder, rolling across the swirling, rain-pitted road, it throws itself out as if their slogans can leap over the heads of the men standing shoulder to shoulder across the road and run off up the hill bearing the message. I ask Maria why they have blocked the road; she says it is to show that the demonstrators can go no further than is allowed, to show who is always in control. I turn to look at the line, standing with their arms folded, their wet uniforms skinned tight onto the flesh of their thighs. Those are women too, I say to sister, and we look at them together, the solid flesh of their bodies, the muscles that bulge in their fatty limbs as they stand immobile against the demonstration. I expect to see the little crowd try its strength against the barrier of metal and authority, and I see it gather and swell forward on a crest of sound as if it will break forward at any moment. But instead they turn around and run off the way they have come. In a moment they have dispersed, disappeared into the crowds on the pavement, and the policewomen have started to hurl barriers back into the vans.

Sister looks down at me in the doorway and says we are going to be late for another appointment; I follow through streets and puddles and the rain sheets into my eyes. Somewhere she turns back to wait for me and then stops. She looks down all over me. My shirt is transparent with rain. In another shop doorway we pause and I huddle my arms over my breasts and glance over the women who hurry the streets, whose breasts and nipples are hidden by their underwear. Sister pushes me through the doorway into the shop and tells me to buy a shirt. In the shop they giggle and point up the stairs to a floor with racks of shirts, and I buy something and put it on behind a curtain and throw myself back out into the street, looking at no one. In the street sister is grinning, and I look again at her and see that she too is wearing the underwear and giving away nothing.

Just now, sitting in the wicker chair and looking down at me on the floor, sister asked whether I had noticed that it was a man's shirt I had bought, that this is a distinction that of course always exists. She will not explain why they pointed me up the stairs to the floor where men are supposed to go to buy their clothes, why they pointed me away from the ground floor where the women shop. But it is not hard to guess that I look like some Lelaki leaving, offspring of a withered test tube, perhaps, and that is why I must shop upstairs. Sister insists only on smiling, and ruffles my hair.

It is almost time to sleep. Sleep is done differently here, because it is hot, because it is the floor that you sleep on. The curling and gathering of yourself that is bed and comfort to me at home, that layered and rounded cocoon, I have abandoned already. I thought they were sleep itself, but I have found that none of these things is necessary. Here you lie down on the wooden boards, lie down flat with your limbs straightened and smoothed out, and you let your flesh loosen off your bones until it settles onto the floor around you. And thus you sleep, still, and laid out. This is a strange country, that sister takes so calmly.

White: Entry#31

As we fly in the streets are empty beneath us, hardly a vehicle moving. It has begun, sister says, clenching her hands on the armrests, the strike is working. I can feel her excitement rushing out ahead of us, rushing out to meet whatever waits for us there, as we shuffle across the hot tarmac. Everyone in the airport building is behaving as if nothing is happening; as if there is no silent paralysed city just beyond the gate. The little turbo-prop reminds me of home, the little hop that they would always be making to the mainland, low enough to see the fish leap. It is always the first flight, the one you make before you can fly the serious, long distances to arrive anywhere else. The airport building is the same, too; prefabricated, with those moulded plastic chairs extruded from the floor; it probably comes from the same Lelaki warehouse.

There are half a dozen taxis outside, basking like sharks in the heat, their doors thrown open. Sister pulls me past them and we start off up the shimmering road. I have been watching her hide her eagerness, giving the airport guards vague smiles, leaving the airport as if she is going to see her cousin in the next street. As we rest beneath a tree, because I can only move a little at a time in the heat, I ask sister what she is expecting, that she can hardly wait. Maybe you are observing, sister says, I am participating, how else shall I find out how things are. As we go on up the road the haze ahead clears into a barricade, banners, the outline of a crowd. We walk slowly towards them, nothing else moving. I am anxious, but sister has only her eager look, unveiled now, as if she is sure of being absorbed into their midst.

112

Now I am lying, as usual, on the floor in front of a fan while sister lies across the room complaining against the unnecessary breeze. I become accustomed to the tension between us until it is no more than the way we are. If we were at home I would say we were dangerous, but we are here. My mind feels raw, abraded, the batch is a cushion that I need between me and strangeness. Perhaps that is the idea, that my mind as it tears apart is more open, a sensitive receiver. I try to bring Tea, Stone, into the room with me; their voices are fitful and thin.

The events of the day telescope and then slide apart in my mind: long stretches of waiting, to reach the end of the road, for something to happen, and then sudden crashes of activity, as sudden as the thunder that breaks intermittently from the clouds that have been lowering overhead throughout the day. Finally reaching the barricade and sister saying certain names with meaning and bringing out her letters of introduction; the suddenness with which we were engulfed by the crowd. And then being put down to wait by the side of the road while the right people are found to fetch us, and the crowd going back at once to its being a barrier, back to the business of waving banners to the still air. Sister hunkers down and leans her head against a wall and smiles while I sit in the dust and feel the sweat spreading into the last corners of my shirt. (Sister tells me, not then while we waited but just now, as she lay on her bed muffled by the mosquito net, that no one here would sit on the ground like that because they would know how difficult it would be to get the dirt out of their trousers. Only a rich woman, with someone else to wash for her, would risk herself like that, on the earth or a bus seat. Sister watches me knocking myself against this country, and every bruise is a confirmation of my unsuitability. I do not tell her that these are measures of her failure to warn me, since she knows this well enough already.)

The car they pick us up in has a thin red rag tied round the radiator grill, messages in the windows. They seem so cheerful and careless, three boys of maybe twenty crushed together in the front seat as if they've come for the ride, the car full of laughter like they had just been let off, let out, and they were breathing freedom neat into their lungs. They remind me, almost, of a half-batch escaped from some farm chore, crossing the island to chase rabbits in the dunes. They are thin, like us, and small, and their eyes shine. They have just heard that something is happening at another barricade, and we are gathered into the car in a rush and taken off across the city; so quiet, no one but the clusters round the barricades on the street. In the centre all the stores are closed, even the bars.

The car stops somewhere and we are running; sister, too, has been taken over by the need to know everything. She is in front of me and so I see nothing except that she stops dead, between one step and the next. We have come out into a square: at the other side is another crowd like the first, but quieter; more of them have pulled their scarves over their faces. Between us and that crowd stand a line of soldiers. They are facing away from us, toward the crowd, and so only the butts of their machine guns peer out from the edge of hip and jacket. The young men walk us slowly, delicately, round the edge of the square, past the soldiers until we can fade into the crowd. From the front the soldiers look almost casual, cradling their weapons. Sister hides me carefully behind a thicker mass of people and points out the army sharpshooters, just a few of them standing to one side against the wall; they also have scarves covering their faces.

I know about excitement; I know the joy of danger, the thrill as your foot slips, running on the cliff path, and you save yourself just barely, both hands clutched desperately into the heather. I know how it feels to go out further than you dare, or ought; and that was how the square was, that afternoon. Exciting, unpredictable, would they maybe shoot, and if they did, would they shoot at me? I could see it in sister too, her eyes dark with staring, hot with the possibility of danger, she was rooted to the spot with it. As we stood, there was a terrible noise and a huge green helicopter was circling the square, a door in its side open and one

114

more gun trailing from the opening, a threatening tentacle brushing the rooftops.

White: Entry#33

This afternoon I washed my clothes – and already they are sitting next to me, dry and folded on the bed. Somehow this brings the power of the sun home to me more directly even than feeling the hot weight of it bearing down on my head, this unfettered power that dries cotton crisp in half an hour. What does it mean that whole peoples are spared the going out into the half-dark noon, feeling the sheets frozen to boards? And yet there is nothing to eat. The three young men eat half what I do, dividing the small fish exactly between them, just allowing themselves a second bowl of rice. I see that they are drinking only to keep me company; from the way sister looks at me, I do not order the second bottle that I want, I do not eat quite all the bananas, but I feel that my hunger has become visible and is sitting beside me, gesturing obscenely. Sister has adjusted her appetite to suit what is available. Maria becomes more protean all the time.

Later yesterday one of the young men explained the mechanics of hunger, an island given over to one crop that it is no longer economic to plant, and the landowners hanging on to the inactive land, arming themselves against those who would farm it to eat. Then he took us out to see the children begging to point up the differences: in the capital it is poverty we have seen, and here it is malnutrition, dry folds of skin, desiccated flesh that hangs away from thin bones like cloth. Sister was overcome with something, all her layers of removal came unhinged, and she began digging in her pockets for sweets and money until the space around her was thick with weak little hands. She does not look like an Islander to these children. They skipped round her pulling her skirts and trying out Lelaki phrases, while I bought sweets off the street sellers and ate them myself one after another. Sister watches me, slipping away from our guides to gorge surreptitiously, stuffing sweets into myself a handful at a time, and she tells me I have been hit by the culture, that I surround myself with food to escape it. I would stop if I could, this disorder disgusting when all around me they are counting grains of rice. I cannot stop.

White: Entry#34

Perhaps a country is like a spring-iced pond, something that you can travel across, always thinking that the grey swirls below you, the brown dart as a fish moves under you, is all – that it is the pond you are seeing. Until there is a crack and fissure, tweaks and shots beneath your feet, and you are sodden waist-deep in it, the cold and the mud and the weight of it. I am lying under the fan, waves of air fighting the sweat that pours out of me, and it is as if I have suddenly found myself under the ice, the reality of the cold gnawing into my bones. My metaphors are all of the cold, the metaphors for pain – they will have to stand. This morning something happened. I knew there was something happening, something other than what was meant to happen, because all the young men left their banners and placards, that they were smearing in red paint ready for the rally, and stood in the hallway around another one that had just driven up, scattering the dust in the road. His face was white from the dust and he breathed in gasps as if he had just run there, from wherever he had come from. Sister and I stood in the doorway of the room where we sleep, watching, sister's hand clenched tight around my arm, as he told his story in a language we did not understand.

Eventually some of the boys in the hall went back to their placards and started again, painting new slogans; I watched one, poised over his blank paper, his brush heavy with a different message, as if he could hardly bear to make the news real by writing it. Our guide told us the story, and I felt sister's hand unclench slowly and drop to her side. He told us that just down the road from here, another town like this one, another strike like this one, there had been fifty or so killed. A similar sort of barricade, the helicopter circling, the milling crowd and the line of soldiers, guns cradled casually in their arms, except that in that

116

town, they had lifted their weapons and shot. And when the crowd fled the soldiers and their weapons had pursued them down the streets, into the cane fields, firing as they came. And now the bodies lay in the summer square and the people, those that were not crouched in the fields still, were crushed into the church, afraid to come out, afraid to drag the dead out of the sun. I began to feel it then, without quite knowing what it was, as if with a sudden crack the ice had parted beneath my feet.

And so this afternoon's rally, that was to have been no more than the necessary gesture of resistance, a cheerful token show of numbers, became an act of witness. Sister and I were taken down to the square by the young men and left by the bandstand, a tiny round thing with a domed roof and pillars. The ones who were going to make speeches were all crowded under the little roof, where a white uniformed band used to play bright witty tunes as dusk fell and carefully-nurtured fountains gushed. The scene comes un-diluted from some universal knowledge of the mechanisms of colonization. I sat on the little wrought iron fence, watching sister, who was trying to mingle with the people but who was being followed by yesterday's children. Then I looked up and saw the helicopter again, circling at the fringes of the crowd. The door was still open, a thin leg, a thin machine gun snout dangling out. It would seem so easy to shoot, that afternoon, the taste of it in the air and the rally organizers gathered so conveniently into a small space in the centre of the square. I no longer felt safe sitting in front of the bandstand so I went and bought mint sweets off a woman sitting in the shade of a tree. Sister tells me that one of this particular brand of sweet dissolved into a can of fizzy drink will get you high; she smiled knowingly as she let this slip, but I doubt she has tried it herself. Maria goes on trying to shock, as if she hopes that something sufficiently alien will cause me to retreat from my task. She wants me to declare that I can see nothing for the strangeness of it all.

When the speeches began we were sat on the roof

of a van while one young man filmed the crowd and another whispered translations. It is very odd to hear eye witness accounts from those who have just managed, maybe an hour ago, to escape from a massacre, instantly translated into your ear in a dry whisper while the crowd, a fraction ahead of you, lets out a great, involuntary groan at some new horrible detail. How the speaker was saved because someone threw himself on top of her and died instead, how no one could tell how many might be lying bleeding to death in the fields where no one dared go to find them. Something, the last thing, happened in the midst of this mass mourning. The helicopter is circling all the time, of course, not too close, just at the edge of sight and hearing. Suddenly a section of the crowd, our section, lifted to its feet and started to run, moving forward in a great wave. The panic was as tangible in the air as tear gas would be, its effect on the brain as inexorable. As the wave of it reached the van I leapt to the ground and crushed myself in with the huddle of people sheltering in the lee of the bonnet. Up there, on the roof, I was a sitting target. I would've run, if I had seen anywhere to go. It was only the not seeing any escape that kept me there.

Nothing happened – the shooting did not start – and gradually the feeling drained away. When it was over, and the running had stopped and someone was leading a rallying call and the crowd had begun, shakily, to sing, I uncurled myself from under the van and noticed that the young men and sister still sat where I had left them, on the roof. I cannot tell whether sister remained where she was because she was paralysed by the panic, or whether she has absorbed somehow the discipline that the young men have that keeps them doing what they are doing in spite of fear, that keeps them from eating in spite of hunger. Their dedication makes my sweaty frailty the more obvious. Sister would I think conclude from this that they are launched upon a struggle that is just and destined for success. But it seems to me one may be fine and upstanding in pursuit of a hopeless cause.

It was when I threw myself off the van that the ice

finally gave beneath me and I found myself in the stinking water, in it all of a sudden with the cold chewing my flesh down to the bone. The nature of the terror was quite different, quite unlike that flash of fear and excitement as I saw the line of soldiers for the first time at the barricade. Different even from that weighing of possibilities that caused me to move away from the bandstand half an hour before. It was only when crouching against the van that I felt the likelihood of sudden arbitrary death. It is an altogether different kind of feeling. Though no doubt those that must learn to live with it can do so, it has me lying beneath the fan with my mind numb from the shock of arctic water.

White: Entry#36

This morning I went out while sister was sat round a table with them gathering the statistics of starvation. How hungry a village must be before it becomes a part of the force, gathering quietly out there in the countryside. I snuck out, against all that they and sister had said, that I should not wander in the town alone. And I felt the fear of it – not just the strangeness of being alone, though that seems no more natural to me, for all the emptiness of home, than it does to the Islanders, who live so close on top of one another – I felt the fear of these particular streets. It was the green helicopters I was fearing, as I walked, that that unearthly noise would reach down out of the sky and pluck me off somewhere. There seem to be watchers wherever I go, people of whose casual enquiries sister has taught me to be cautious. It is her assumption that their interest is dangerous, that they are the helicopter's grounded tentacles. When they ask where we are going she tells them we are travelling just down the street, when they ask where we have come from she gestures vaguely in the direction of the airport, or the cafe where we have been sitting. Sometimes they seem to insist too much, and I catch her suspiciousness and turn my face from their hidden cameras, their veiled, searching looks. But if they are all, indeed, the spies sister fears, then the number of them must be unimaginably vast, for they stand at every street corner, under every tree.

Why was I going out, when sister had said that I should not? That is hardly something that we do, except as the smallest of children, experimenting to see what it's like, to go against yourself. But we break down here, sister — Maria — and I. Our certainties are blurred as she becomes more sharply defined, a being quite separate from me. Can I even assume that our interests are in common? But I cannot say what that would mean, how we could have interests that were not. So I walked out into the steam of the morning. It had just rained and the bushes and trees hanging over roadside fences steamed in the sun. The market has begun again, the shops are open after the strike, but still there seems to be a pall of quiet over the streets, as if they have not yet quite forgotten what it is like, when the whole of a city stops.

On my way I stopped and bought bread; at every bakery I stopped and bought rolls or sticky buns, more rolls. And as I walked on I tore them out of their bags and stuffed them into my mouth as if a huge importunate worm stood in my throat groaning for nourishment. Nothing seems to fill the gnawing hunger, it swallows and opens its mouth once more, always ravening. So I arrived at the main plaza, a sugary taste to my lips from the sweet bread. The children had abandoned their begging and were playing on the knobby grass in the shade of the trees, turning somersaults and cartwheels on their bone-thin limbs. I sat on a bench and waited, as if I expected something to happen. But it was quiet, and eventually I laid myself out along the bench and went to sleep.

When I opened my eyes there was a young woman squatting in the grass on the other side of the path. She smiled and went on considering me, her gaze moving slowly over every inch of my body. She was wearing a shirt and trousers not so different from my own; she looked altogether similar, it came to me, the same sort of shape, more solid than the Islanders tend to be. You would say that they are usually small and dark and willowy, especially the women, despite being so mixed, where she was stocky like many of the Baba-i are, as I am. Though not, of course, blond.

We looked at one another, and I wondered what she was seeing. She sat down beside me on the bench. "Lelaki?" "Baba-i," I said. She grinned, but vaguely, as if I were making a distinction which had no meaning for her or in which she was not interested. Then she wrote her name and address on a piece of paper and gave it to me. So I borrowed her pen and wrote down mine, a place thousands of miles away of which she cannot have heard. She took it from me politely, looked pointedly at her address, smiled at me some more and then went away. I watched her loping diagonally across the square. I sat on the bench for a while trying to understand who I might seem to be to her, coming across me slumped across a seat in the midday; why I might be worth stopping to look at, worth waking with the power of a stare, worth the risk of a name given to a stranger.

White: Entry#37

I am sitting at the desk in our room, waiting for sister to come out of her briefing, losing account of time, watching the sudden flurries of wind tear at the leaves I do not recognize in the street outside, the squalls of rain that thud down, and stop, hardly cooling the air. And I watch the sun, which I suspect I have never seen before, so other is it to the thin thing I have lifted my face to in the lee of the rocks of home. And it comes to me that there is something that I recognized in her smile, that at home I would have understood straight away. She smiled at me as we do when we acknowledge the completeness of our understanding with one another, and when we mean to be sexual. I have come here, of course, expecting the eyes of the women to be turned elsewhere. And they are so clearly turning within a different circle of expectation that there is no point of contact; I do not find myself expecting it. I find myself wondering how warmth is possible across the gulf that divides these men and these women. Sister is urbane and assures me that the rest of the world is exhilarated by incompatibility and misunderstanding, that our security and knowledge of one another would make them feel unbearably overlooked. And even if one of these women were to look at me, it could only be for that same dangerous, incomplete contact, the thought of which suggests to me something not immediately pleasurable or intelligent, like walking barefoot across a thistled pasture. So I have been apart, have been keeping myself apart. I can wait. Sometimes sister and I talk, but what we talk about is not each other but the absent batch. We take it for granted that nothing else is worth having, we are sexual perfectionists and prefer nostalgia to some passing substitute. Perhaps I ought not to be surprised that this young woman looks at me, smiling into my eyes, that one woman can be propositioned by another in the main square, here just as well as anywhere else. But it means that she cannot know who I am.

Sister has just arrived and was unimpressed. She asked me what else I expected, looking as I do here. There is a bit of mirror in the hall and I went and looked at myself. I looked hot and rumpled and solid. Sister opened the door and gestured at the reflection; you look like what they call a tomboy here, she said, that is what they call them. She said the Islands are full of them – the line of policewomen standing thigh to thigh in the city – and of course they would recognize me. What are they recognizing, I asked her, if they see me and not her. Sister admitted that she was hiding from them. She said that she needs to be taken seriously if anyone is to speak to her, and that no one takes tomboys seriously. I can survive, she said, in her wake, and because I can just listen to the answers to the questions that her disguise enables her to ask.

Sister told me that tomboys are supposed to feel themselves born to be men – this is why they dress differently from other women – and to strive to be as like them as possible. We had to laugh. Sister became quite sick with laughter and had to stuff mosquito net into her mouth to make herself stop. All evening she has been saying, so you want to be a man, at intervals, and starting us giggling insanely. It's a joke that no one else understands, naturally. So we shall have to stop laughing soon.

* * *

Maria: Entry#479

Perhaps you will have some measure of the unattainable out of this, oh wise ones. Little sister here is drunk with misunderstanding, bloated with it. Of course she is well trained and knows perfectly that she is confused, but self-knowledge doesn't drain the bloat out. It makes for despair or risibility.

Not knowing what's going on never stopped anybody from action ... but even the Lelaki seem curiously inert. Insofar as I can get over my fear of their mere presence (and perhaps I shouldn't, they must be wherever they are for a reason), I can't see that they're pursuing even information with any energy. You wouldn't be wanting us to fill the gap, surely. It isn't a vacuum. I could point out, if I were not in danger of being accused of teaching a Librarian to suck eggs, the Islanders are cheerfully engaged in their very own affairs in the midst of this gallery of watchers. Much good may it do them, I know; I also know, how not, that it is the watchers upon whom I should also be fastening my dissecting gaze. Well, perhaps I can't do that either, perhaps they too are opaque to me, and I'm tired of speculation, my mind is numbed by it. What anchor point should I imagine or construct for us here? It isn't often that I feel an affection for physical labour, but just now I could be glad even for the fish station, even in winter, I would even gut fish for a week and not complain about how the stench envelops you until it seems to be coming from the inside out, as if you're generating it from every pore and orifice. And don't tell me I don't mean it. I have lost even an imagination of a sense of place. Fish stink would be somewhere to start. By the odour of rotting marine flesh shall I know myself. Another repressive bleat (not to get onto them again, though there's a smell, now, that lingers); culture shock, you

123

say wearily, disbelievingly, muttering to each other and raising your eyebrows. Yes, sisters, still. Always.

They are so complete, here, that is what undoes us. Their belief in possibility is infinite. There was a woman here yesterday that I spoke to. The organizer in her village had just been vanished – no body, but no sign of her alive, either – and she was taking her place. Aren't you afraid, I said, and she merely looked at me reprovingly. Supposing they pick you up and torture you, I said, aren't you afraid of telling. She gave me this pitying smile: we expect more of ourselves than that, she said. That I find such faith dangerous, or misplaced, or faintly inhuman is of course an indication of my inevitable distance from her, but it is also about *her* distance from *me*. She is cocooned, and we are dancing on the edge, trying to look significant and marginal all at the same time. Maybe we even could be significant, even if it wasn't deliberate (and surely we are never deliberate) – but would it matter? Would it matter, if the Islanders didn't believe in our significance? It would be hard, wouldn't it, if we finally resolved on action only to find that it had no reality outside our own minds.

But I am against everything. I am against everything, including especially your taking any account of such random fractious messages as you may be getting from us in the Islands. To an even greater extent I am against our indulging in fantasies of power and intervention, so I'm not sure where that leaves me. It leaves me preferring that we indulge in fantasies of waste and inertia, perhaps.

Chapter 3

[Taken from the Library of Baba-i: records of the Librarians' meeting on the question of the Islands.]

Loti: Tell me what will happen. Tell me what you see.

Grace: Appearances that are deceptive. Here I can sit on the sheep-cropped grass, the sand of the bay spread beneath me a simple white, the sea blue. I can lift my face to the sun and feel its warmth; I need not feel the wind pushing at my hair, pushing into my ears. You have seen it, in summer, the colours blue and white, the colours of a tropical island, hot sand and warm sea. And yet if I were to scramble down the dune, take off my shoes and walk across the sand, if I were to put my foot into that blue, blue water. How quickly the illusion of heat would vanish. The water is iceberg-fed and eager to freeze, it will numb me in a moment.

      What is going to happen is what has happened before.

Atis: Perhaps they will refuse. To see only our summer, even if we acknowledge its cold, is not to see enough. I can imagine more. I can imagine what lies further south, across the water. I can see the blizzard dark that never lifts, the cold that settles closer and closer. Even in the long light of summer, especially in the long light of summer, I can remember and fear the coming of dusk at noon, I can imagine how much more terrible the cold and dark

125

must be there, further south still. Perhaps they will have to refuse.

Grace: They are not really offered a choice. Think of the inducements. Think of what they'll be offered. An image of prosperity, of heaven realized here on earth. The image carefully adjusted to fit in with Island expectations and desires, plenty of well-fed smiling brown children, all with shoes on their feet. Every village a haven of peace and contentment now that poverty has been banished. No more civil turmoil; everyone agreeing with everyone else. Think of the posters going up on roadside hoardings all over, gigantic three times lifesize visions of happiness marching into every Island brain.

I wonder where the women will go, this time. I know that this is not what you want to hear, but I have to be bleak.

Loti: You have to be bleak? Why do you think that the Lelaki will not let them have women? I need reasons, not bleakness out of habit.

Grace: They may have them to start with, but how can it last, with that shining example before them? There's only one proper way to do it. It will be less tidy in the Islands, that's all, with no convenient distant territory to which to parcel off the unwanted remnants. Of course they'll do it differently, the Lelaki aren't above learning from their mistakes. They'll have to make those women believe, make them embrace the new world with stars in their eyes. It will be presented to them as a chance that they must have faith enough to grasp. They must take up the challenge and place themselves alongside the men, in the vanguard. How can they refuse, even though it will be in vain, even though the end is inevitable.

It's logical. It's not that it doesn't pain me to think of those women thinking they hold the means of a new life in their hands, of the despair that faces them.

Loti: But they are not the same women as those that came here. They are different, a different time, a different place.

Grace: They are prey to the same delusions. The same world, fundamentally, conspires to delude them. You are deceived by superficial modifications in their status.

Loti: You see the same thing everywhere, that is your position? Place is contingent. I need more than this. Come on, Atis.

Atis: Another story. Come with me, then. A short enough journey: we are in the cold and the dark, in the featureless white wastes of the antarctic. Here the only sound is made by the wind in your ears, a howling and perpetual wind so much worse than our own; after a certain time you will cease to hear it, however, and the world will seem silent. All about you the snow whirls and the ice creaks and shifts on itself. It seems as if you share this place only with death and solitude and the endless wind. The rest is hibernation, hardly different, different only in that, should this dark ever lighten, there is some abstract promise of motion and warmth. The flower seeds beneath your feet, far down in the snow, await the changing of the season, insensate and safe. The bears, unconscious, inert, have long since abandoned the challenge of this cold. In their sleep they consume themselves; if they have not eaten to sufficient excess the spring will be too long in coming and they will not wake. The seals swam away an age ago, so agile and easy through the water, quickly before the ice caught them, following the fish to warmer waters. They will not return until it is all over, this suffering.

        Why is it that only the penguins do not acknowledge their limitations? Why must they stay here, here where survival is surely beyond possibility? Surely it is more than should be asked of any species, it is beyond

127

the bounds of endurance. Here they stand, stolid in the dark. Motionless, the eggs laid so carelessly in the summer light nestled on their feet to keep infant fragility from the seeping death of the ice. It is against reason, your mind revolts against it, this act of endurance. Months, motionless on the ice in the dark, their heads towards the horizon where, finally, the sky will begin to lighten. Where, at last, the sun will rise.

They will go underground. They will go into the hills.

Loti: It's true, there are hiding places. It would be impossible to search the mountains.

Grace: That is no solution. What would they be doing? Watching the world change, down there in the valleys. Without power, stealing chickens to survive.

Atis: It would not matter. They would be waiting. They would be alive. They wouldn't need a reason beyond that.

Grace: Everyone needs hope of some kind.

Loti: Oh, except you. It's no good you trying to understand Atis' point of view. I wish you'd leave the synthesis to me.

Atis: You have a monopoly on a global perspective, do you. The hell with synthesis. You sound heady from all this power, Loti – all this power to make unenforceable decisions.

Grace: Quite. After all, whatever we do makes not the slightest difference to the Islands.

Loti: We also have the technology. And we could give it to the women of the Islands, should they happen to be holed up safely in the hills. That would make a difference, Grace.

Grace: Sure, it would make a difference. But don't you think it would make all the difference to the men as well? How could the Lelaki leave them there, growing and waiting in the mountains? They would have to clear them out, blow the mountains apart, flush them out at whatever cost, raze the mountains to the ground if need be. They'd pick the women off gradually, it would be very messy. They wouldn't be allowed to survive once they weren't harmless any longer. And if they're harmless, they're not going to survive. Simple.

Loti: I admit, I'm confused. It is easy to be confused when your way of life is founded on uncertainty. There are times when our life resembles too closely that of a tribe whose numbers have been reduced beyond all hope of revival by some invasive act of violence — war, disease, they are the same, usually. The last members live on, because it is so difficult to die, because dying requires effort. They age, knowing that they represent something that is over, that they have no meaning. And because it is hard to live like that, they take on a listless look, they become shadowy and inert. You don't have to tell me that I exaggerate: but this exists all right, a sort of ghost, a shadow in the background of our awareness.

Choosing is so hard for us, too hard. We need a traditional ground for action, something that is buried so deep that it is almost beyond question, so that even if it is questioned the imprint is still there. It is too much, this freedom, being who we choose to be, it's paralysing. Three women juggling possibilities of enormous size; the absurdity itself is paralysing.

Atis: There are mountains and wildernesses at home, too.

Grace: At home? What do you mean, at home?

Atis: You know what I mean, Grace. Literally, even, Lelaki was our home once, it was where we came from.

Grace: We have to take on that guilt? Outcasts don't have to take on that guilt. We're as far from them as we can be.

Loti: As we can be — how far is that?

Grace: What about these wildernesses, from which you say you came?

129

Atis: Women might survive there, that was what I
        was thinking. I was thinking of small, quiet,
        overgrown trails in the hills, the friendly
        sounds of a familiar dawn, the easy stride of a
        traveller who knows every inch of the ground.
Grace: They got rid of them, generations ago. Sys-
        tematically removed, every last one of them.
        I'm sure you've read what it says in the
        library, it's very well documented. And since
        then there's been no trace, not even a myth.
        Not one old crone up in the hills eating babies
        story to frighten the children with. And no one
        loses their chickens there, or their machine
        guns, either. They aren't there. If they were
        there would be traces.
Atis: Not necessarily.
Grace: You take unreasonableness too far, Atis. Even
        for unreasonableness. What use is that?
Loti: It might be no use at all, or it might be the
        whole point. But I think you are both just
        arguing for the sake of it. Hot air. I give up.

[At this point the records show that one of the
Librarians left the room. Her notes, made on return,
indicate that on leaving the building she followed a
sheep track around the side of a hill. It was summer;
the grass was springy under her feet. The ruts of the
track were sown with minute purple flowers. She felt
disoriented, having left when her rôle required that
she stay, when it was her function to persuade others
to stay. Her feet crushed flowers, releasing a sharp
scent. She continued to walk until she reached the lee
of the hill, noting that here the grass seemed to flicker,
silvering where the wind caught and flattened it. She
records that she found a slight hollow in the ground,
where she lay down, face to the earth. The ground was
cold beneath her with the chill that never quite leaves,
even in summer. The grass was sharp, and it dug
through the loose summer weave of her clothing. It
was not her expectation, she explained, that the earth
would provide anything in the way of mystic communication; her impression was that she was instead

*made aware anew of the harshness and unyielding
nature of the landscape.]*

When she returned, Grace and Atis had moved
onto the porch, where the glass intensified the heat of
the sun and kept off the wind. They were dividing a
small cheese between them.

"You left," Grace said, around a soft lump of
cheese.

"I'm sorry."

"While you were gone, we decided to try a little
synthesis of our own." Atis giggled, and licked the
corners of her mouth.

"You did? I suppose we may as well break all the
rules at once." Loti leaned against the glass wall, her
back to the sun.

"Yes. You see, I think about endurance all the time,
how it's possible under any conditions if there's
reason enough. And Grace sees loss of power, women
being marginalized – something gradual but inevitable. You see?"

"No." Loti shifted her shoulder against the glass.
She had grass down her back, or perhaps it was
rheumatism.

"Well, if we put the two things together, they might
mean survival, survival in small, endangered groups.
Maybe it means that even in Lelaki we survived. If
only for a while."

"In this famous wilderness?"

"You can be very literal, sister. Perhaps the
wilderness is only a metaphor. Perhaps in the Islands
it will be possible in the cities, too, as well as further
from the centres of power where control is weak."

Loti walked over to the table and sat down. She
reached out a finger to the fragments of cheese that
clung to the plate, "And do we take them what we
have?"

Grace nodded. "If they ask. We must let them know
that the possibility is there. Theirs if they want it."

"You decided – without me."

"You may survive it."

* * *

131